MURDER BY HANGING

NORFOLK COZY MYSTERIES

KEITH FINNEY

Keith Finney - Author

AN INVITATION

Welcome to your invitation to join my Readers' Club.

Receive free, exclusive content only available to members including short stories, character interviews and much more.

To join, click on the link towards the end of this book and you're in!

THE HANGING TREE

Sally Evans struggled to keep with up her jogging mate, Jessica Brownlow, on the muddy forest track.

"It's okay for you, Jessica. You're not the one with a passenger on board."

As Sally leant forward, with a hand resting on each knee to catch her breath, she glimpsed her friend feign indifference.

"It's more likely that second double latte from Baldwin's has done for you. I told you to take it easy."

Sally wafted a hand in playful defiance and chose not to acknowledge the mischievous smile spreading across Jessica's cheeks.

"Anyway, you're only twelve weeks gone! And you were the one that insisted on doing this route. We could have done the old railway run in half the time."

Sally straightened her torso, and hands on hips, took a deep breath.

"I said we could do this route if *you* wanted to. You belted across the village green tout suite, which by my reckoning, settled the matter."

A score draw now established, the pair took in the quiet beauty of Stanton Woods. A heavy frost coated the bronze-tinged leaves in a white coating of crystalline ice. Backlit by the low morning sun, Sally thought the effect was breathtaking.

"Crisp winter mornings are magical, aren't they?"

Jessica nodded as a shaft of sunlight pierced a gap in the tree canopy, hitting the ground at a low angle just ahead of them.

"Beats making the beds and washing dirty socks. Talking of which, we'd better get a move on. Tell you what, the first to the clearing gets to choose which track we use back to the village," said Jessica.

Keen to gain the advantage, Sally set off before her friend had finished speaking.

She turned to see Jessica hanging back, kicking aside frosted leaves from the track and guessed her friend didn't want to push too hard in case she fell and injured the baby.

Thought so.

Before long, Sally arrived at the clearing to claim victory knowing Jessica had engineered the result.

About to let out a whoop of victory, her attention was suddenly grabbed by the dreadful sight ahead.

She wanted to scream; no sound would come.

She stood rigid, her head cocked to one side and tilted upwards.

"Good God."

Sally hadn't noticed her friend arrive. At her feet lay a wide, short log on its side resting on the thick carpet of leaf mould.

"Come away," said Jessica as she placed a comforting arm around her friend's shoulder.

"Nothing we can do for him now, poor devil."

The limp figure slowly swung from side to side in a gentle breeze.

"How does someone end up desperate enough to do that, Jessica?" Her hushed tone and extended arm reinforced the point.

"He must've been so cold and lonely. By the looks of things, he's been there all night. See the frost on the rope? Heavens, it's awful."

Sally accepted Jessica's guiding arm in turning her away from the body, towards a fallen tree on the opposite side of the clearing.

"Take the weight off your feet. We need to get the police up here. Will you be all right if I go for help?"

Sally nodded, dusted a coating of frost from the fallen tree, her back towards the body.

"I'll be fine. Just be as quick as you can."

———

LYN BLACKTHORN, head teacher of Stanton Parva Junior School was, as usual, late as she drove out of the village towards Norwich.

The agenda for the monthly meeting of heads didn't inspire her. But at least it was a chance to catch up with old friends and have a communal moan.

Good to get a bit of group therapy.

Keen to make up time, Lyn pressed the accelerator of her Mini Clubman, entering open countryside only too aware of the dangers posed by the narrow lanes and unkempt drainage ditches.

They left little room for error.

Rounding a shallow bend to the right, Lyn reacted in an instant to a figure standing on the verge, waving her arms.

Once stopped she wound down the window. She recognised the woman, concern etched on her face.

"Jessica, what's the matter?"

"Lyn, thank heavens it's you. There's a body; we need the police."

Lyn's mind raced as she made sense of Jessica's breathless words.

"A body? Has there been an accident?"

Jessica shook her head as she turned back in the direction of the clearing.

"An accident? No, I don't think so. He's hanging from a tree."

Lyn's expression turned to shock.

People don't hang themselves in Stanton Parva.

Her momentary lapse of concentration passed and reverted to type, focusing on what needed doing. Taking her mobile from the dashboard she pressed the emergency services shortcut.

"And Sally, she's pregnant... and..."

Lyn frowned.

"Sally? Pregnant? What's that got to do with—"

She allowed Jessica to interrupt.

"Oh dear, I'm sorry. I mean, well... We were jogging and..."

Lyn nodded.

At the same time her call connected.

"Police and ambulance please. I think there's been a suicide by hanging."

After giving the operator their location, Lyn turned back to Jessica

"I get it. Jessica, is..."

Yes, she's in the clearing with the, you know..."

"SALLY, how are you? Jessica has told me what happened."

"At last. Thought you'd got lost."

In truth, less than ten minutes had passed.

Lyn turned towards the tree and walked with a measured pace until she stood just in front of the man. His facial features distorted, but she still recognised him.

"It's Ethan Baldwin."

Her two companions stared wide eyed at the lifeless figure.

"Ethan? No, it can't be. I saw him just the other day; he seemed fine. It's awful... and we didn't even recognise the poor man."

Lyn gestured for Sally to retake her seat.

"I'm afraid so, Sally. You're both in shock. Why would you recognise him? Look at the state he's in."

Lyn noticed her unwitting invitation for the pair to once again view the corpse had an unexpected calming effect on Jessica and Sally. She sensed looking at the body helped them accept what had happened.

Lyn encouraged the women to talk about their memories of a man the whole village knew and respected as their church warden.

The interlude didn't last long.

Lyn heard the rustle of leaves from behind. She turned to see a familiar figure.

Lord, what an irritating man you are.

"You seem to make a habit of finding bodies, Miss Blackthorn," said Detective Inspector Riley.

As he spoke, he gestured for two police constables to tape off the patch of ground surrounding Ethan's corpse.

"Please step back, ladies. I won't have the scene contaminated."

Lyn bristled. She found Riley's tone officious and lacking emotion, save for his own self-importance.

She refused to be bated. Normally respectful of serving officers, she had little time for this one.

"That will be Ms Blackthorn to you, Detective Inspector."

She knew he detested women getting the better of him. Lyn also knew Riley hated being told to use the noun because he couldn't say it without sounding like a bee with anger management issues.

Now there's a man in need of a polyp removal surgery if ever I saw one.

The mental image of an assertive nurse removing streams of cotton wool packing from Ryley's swollen nostrils after the operation appealed to Lyn's sense of humour.

Riley ignored her instruction.

"And no meddling this time. And that goes for your man friend."

Lyn watched as Riley crossed his double-breasted overcoat in an exaggerated fashion and did up fake horn buttons against the chilly breeze.

Lyn smiled and pressed another of Riley's buttons.

"I presume you are talking about Anthony Norton D'Arcy, the Lord Stanton?"

Her assertive tone caused Riley to wince as her expert shot found its target.

"Whatever," said the detective, making no attempt to disguise his petulance.

Lyn pressed home her advantage.

"Well, Mr Riley. You can be sure that if Lord Stanton, or

I, find anything of interest, you'll be the first to know about it."

She guessed her friendship with the Earl of Stanton's son fed Riley's inferiority complex. She could also see her use of the detective inspector's civilian title added to his already bad mood, not helped by the stifled chuckle of the two constables on the other side of the clearing.

"Get on with your job, you two," barked Riley.

Lyn watched his face turn puce. His subordinates attempted to stifle their laughter. They turned around and made themselves busy adjusting the police tape for no other reason than to break eye contact with their superior.

There stands a man only a mother could love, thought Lyn.

"Hı. Listen, Tina, can you give my apologies to the heads' meeting. Just say something came up, and I'll contact them later to explain."

"Okay, I'll sort it, but it must have been important for you to pull out? Are you all right?"

Lyn conjured a mental image of Ethan's hanging from the tree.

"Yes, yes, I'm fine. Let's just say it's been a difficult morning, Tina. Anyway, yes, on my way back. I'll tell you all about it then. See you in about twenty minutes."

Lyn terminated the call without waiting for a response, brought the Mini to life and roared off, laying a trail of mud from behind the front wheels as she transitioned from soil to tarmac.

As she entered Stanton Parva, Lyn noticed half a dozen locals huddled around the entrance to St. Mary's, the church where Ethan had served as warden for decades.

Suppose I'd better break the news to the vicar.

Lyn pulled into the small gravel car park separated from the ancient graveyard by a low flint wall. Locking the Mini, she made her way to the waiting locals.

"Don't suppose you've seen Ethan," said Mary Chadwick, a longstanding member of the church choir.

Oh no, what do I say?

She deflected the question, her teacher training coming in handy for once.

"I was just going to ask you the same question about Reverend Morton. Is he around?"

Lyn's measured informality did the trick in sidestepping the parishioner's question.

"Wouldn't be waiting in the cold if he'd bothered to turn up on time," said a man with a red nose and watery eyes.

"The reverend should have arrived half an hour ago. It's not at all like him to be late," another added.

Great, a dead church warden and a missing vicar, thought Lyn.

MEMORIES

Lyn strolled from the dining room of Stanton Hall and into the conservatory with her closest friend, Lord Anthony Stanton.

She knew his title was only a courtesy designation because his father was the Earl of Stanton but sounded impressive to her nonetheless.

"Lovely supper, Ant. Now that your parents have gone up, there's something I want to talk to you about."

Lyn watched her best friend tense. She realised immediately he'd got the wrong end of the stick. About to rephrase her sentence, Ant got in first.

"The assessment, you mean?"

Lyn hadn't meant to get him to talk about that just yet. Nevertheless, she could see he needed to.

"So how did it go?" From your expression, I'm guessing not too well?"

Lyn watched on as three deep furrows creased Ant's forehead.

"Officially, it's a medical discharge. Unofficially, they're letting me go but have put me on the reserve list for any special-operations stuff that might come up closer to home. As usual, the army wants it both ways."

Lyn made for her favourite wicker chair and looked out over the rolling pasture sloping gently down to Stanton Broad.

"Well, you either have post traumatic stress disorder or you don't. What do they want from you?"

Turning to face Ant, her voice betrayed simmering anger at the way the army had behaved towards him.

"They reckon that while I can't cope with battlefield conditions, I am capable of undercover stuff in the UK. Simple as that."

"And your parents?"

She noticed Ant take a sharp intake of breath.

"Problematic, that one. I've decided to keep quiet for the time being. I don't want Mum and Dad to think they've forced me into it."

Lyn cocked her head to one side.

"Forced you into what?"

He took several seconds to respond.

I'm coming back for good to manage the Hall and estate. Someone's got to sort the mess out, and I'm not having another estate manager ripping us off, like Narky Collins."

The mention of Narky set off a tangle of emotions as she recalled their recent investigation into his murder and discovery that he had been generating false invoices for years, bleeding Ant's parents dry.

Distracted for a few seconds, Lyn finally turned her attention back to Ant. She surmised from her friend's deter-mined tone that discussing his future helped bury less-palatable memories of his military service.

Lyn's eyes widened at the prospect of having him home. *At last*, she thought.

"When will you tell them?"

Lyn worked hard to keep her excitement in check.

"In a day or two. You could see how knackered they both were at supper."

Lyn smiled. She admired how he fussed over his parents and contrasted it with the difficult relationship she had with her own mother and father.

"But there will have to be changes. We have to get this place paying for itself if it's to have any future."

Lyn let out a throaty laugh.

"Tell me about it. I got soaked when I brought over the chocolate cake I baked. Your stupid porch roof leaked water all over me."

"My point exactly!"

Lyn watched Ant laugh and assumed he was visualising the bedraggled state she had arrived in.

"Your mum and dad will love it. You know how long they've wanted you back but wouldn't have put you under pressure by saying so..."

Lyn hesitated.

"Especially because you're... the only one left?"

Neither needed to speak further on the matter.

"Anyway, what have you been up to today? You said you had something to tell me. Not more boring school stuff, I hope?"

Lyn rested back in the wicker chair and lazily wagged a finger at him.

"Well, if you're not interested..."

Ant returned Lyn's gesture.

"None of that head-teacher stuff from you, young lady."

Lyn refused to rise to his tease. Instead, her smile broadened as she gestured for him to sit on the chair opposite.

She recounted the discovery of Ethan's body and the curious case of the missing vicar.

"And to cap it all, Riley's certain it's suicide and had the cheek to warn us both off."

"THE THING IS, ANT," said Lyn as they inspected the tree Ethan had hung from, "Ethan was crippled with arthritis. There's no way he could have strung a rope over that branch, let alone haul a heavy stump, climb onto it, and kick it away to hang himself."

Lyn watched as Ant took in the scene. He stood behind a cordon of blue-and-white, plastic tape with the repeated message: Police Do Not Cross.

"It certainly must have taken some effort; I'll give you that. He must have been, what, three feet off the ground?"

She noticed Ant give the fallen tree stump, Ethan had used to stand on, a backwards glance and frown as he walked to the far side of the clearing. He turned, crouched, and fixed his gaze on the ground six feet from where the church warden's body had hung. She knew he was in battle-field detective mode as he forensically surveyed every detail of the scene.

"That's interesting."

Lyn looked on, knowing from past experience not to interrupt his train of thought.

"Look at this."

Lyn obeyed his direction to join him.

"See those two faint lines?"

Lyn followed Ant's pointing finger but saw nothing. Closing one eye then the other to get a different perspective made no difference.

"Nope. Don't see anything except mud and leaves."

Lyn almost fell backwards in surprise as Ant clapped his hands.

"Exactly, but not all leaves are the same, you know. Do what I do, and you'll see it."

Lyn watched as Ant moved his upper body and head from side to side while keeping his feet fixed to the spot.

"If you catch the light you can just see two narrow lines leading out of the clearing towards the main road."

Ant pointed to emphasise his point.

Lyn copied Ant's technique. It worked.

"Good Lord, yes, I see. So you agree it wasn't suicide?"

Ant was already following the tracks.

Thirty seconds later, Lyn looked on as Ant studied a small patch of mud.

"What?"

"Bald tyres, Lyn. Poor maintenance I'd say. But it could be anything that's been down here. Not proof of murder."

Continuing along the track, the pair soon came to a gravelled area accessed off a main road from the village.

"It's used as a car park now. Nothing official or anything, but the landowner has never had any problem with the locals using it."

Lyn broke into a broad smile as she finished speaking.

Ant laughed. It was his family's land.

"Shame the kids don't appreciate it though," replied Ant.

Both looked up at a line of broken branches.

"I seem to remember us doing much the same when we were kids, Lyn."

She remembered happy summers larking about in the woods with Ant and his older brother.

Seems like half a dozen lifetimes away.

Lyn looked at her watch.

"Oh Lord. Great times, Ant. But if I don't get back to school for year-six choir practice, my secretary will have my guts for garters, to say nothing of the kids. Come on, Ant."

With that she was off heading at pace back to the Mini.

"I'll make my own way back to the village, Lyn. It'll save you time not having to drop me off."

"Talk later, then, Ant. We can decide what to do next, yes?"

MEMORIES of his brother Greg and the sight of the church sparked a need to pay his respects. He spent five minutes in quiet contemplation in front of his older brother's headstone.

I wonder if the church has changed much since...

Pushing open the medieval oak door of the east entrance kept in place by ancient iron-strap hinges, Ant paused to admire the faded flags hanging from nave walls. He knew each represented a regiment that had fought during the World Wars. As he walked forward, lost in his own world, his attention was drawn to the diminutive frame of a young woman sitting in the front pew.

He quietly passed then turned around to face her. Ant noticed the young woman's pale complexion and watched tears make slow, quiet progress down her cheeks.

Ant readied himself as she looked up at him. Before he could introduce himself, she spoke.

"He was always nice to me. Why would he do that?"

Her voice started to break.

Ant guessed who she was talking about. Nevertheless, he didn't want to get it wrong.

"Who?"

Ant studied her face.

No older than eighteen, I'd say.

Ant watched as she lowered her gaze until it was fixed firmly on the burnt-orange-and-cream-glazed floor tiles.

"Ethan."

He hesitated for a few seconds.

"Ah, yes. I heard. So sad. Dreadful thing to have happened."

Ant made no attempt to press the matter. He didn't need to.

"We could talk to one another about whatever we wanted. Even though he was a lot older than me. But lately he was strange. I think he was worried about something. I think someone was giving him grief. Wanted something he had. He wouldn't tell me. That wasn't like Ethan. Do you think they hurt him?"

Her assertions took Ant by surprise.

Why was she thinking that way? More to the point, why would she be opening up to a stranger in an otherwise empty church?

Ant watched on helplessly as she broke down. She sobbed, tears streaming down her flushed cheeks.

Poor girl. What the hell do I do now?

A voice came to Ant's rescue.

"Samantha. It must be awful for you, but the church is here to provide comfort."

Ant turned to see the reverend walking towards them.

"Anthony, how good to see you, though it has been some time since we've seen you on a Sunday, hasn't it?"

The vicar spoke quietly. Ant thought his gentle Irish lilt fitted the moment perfectly. But he wasn't sure how to respond. He'd never been one for religion even though he felt something that seemed to help when Greg died, without quite understanding why.

Wish I knew what to believe.

As the vicar took a seat next to the teenager, Ant seized the opportunity to escape.

Best leave it to the professionals.

As he walked down the narrow tarmac path towards the road, he heard a commotion coming from the church car park.

A familiar figure stood in the near distance.

Detective Inspector Riley.

"I want to talk to you," Riley shouted.

Ant smiled. He could see the redoubtable Phyllis had other ideas.

"Don't you ignore me, Sergeant. You splashed Betty and me when you came screeching across the path. In my day, bobbies had respect for people. The only thing you seem to care about is getting to the chippie before it closes. Disgraceful."

Ant watched in amusement as Riley tried in vain to escape his tormentors.

"Madam, I..."

Ant grinned and reckoned the icy stare Phyllis gave the hapless policeman could freeze the life out of a snowman.

"Don't call me madam. Such a rude man. I'm a respectable married woman not the owner of a knocking shop."

Her lifelong companion, Betty, nodded. Ant knew she always agreed with Phyllis because it made for an easy life. Emboldened, she started to speak.

"But Phyllis, your Albert's been dead these last twenty yea—"

"Never mind that now, Betty," interrupted Phyllis

without looking at her friend. "So what are you going to do about my dirty tights, Sergeant?"

Ant sensed Riley had had enough, which served only to increase the comedic value.

"Madam, I made no such accusation, and I am not a sergeant. In fact, I am a detective inspector, and what exactly do you expect me to do about your tights, wash them myself?"

Ant knew Riley was now in for a fall and could easily predict Phyllis' response.

"You dirty, dirty man," shrieked Phyllis.

Yep, thought so.

By now, a small group of curious onlookers had gathered.

"Keep your hands off my tights. What a horrible little sergeant you are. Let me tell you…"

Ant watched as the tirade continued with Phyllis threatening the hapless Riley with her sizable handbag then seized the moment and slipped from the policeman's clutches, while the detective was otherwise engaged fending off a fake-crocodile-skin battering ram. Waving at the policeman, he observed Riley almost bursting with frustration in his unsuccessful effort to placate Phyllis and stop him escaping.

3

A FISH SUPPER

Restoring vintage cars came close to an obsession for Ant. One make dazzled him in particular: a Morgan.

Tonight he was ably assisted by his mechanic friend.

"Amazing machines aren't they, Fitch?"

The two men, each dressed in a blue overall that had seen better days, stood side by side as they admired the sorry remains of a once majestic 1936 4/4 Roadster.

Ant knew that to an outsider, the mangle of bits and pieces scattered around the barn floor might seem fit only for the skip.

He ogled the treasure with the wide-eyed amazement of a true believer. To him, the unkempt mixture of metal and wood represented the best of British engineering.

Ant knew Fitch felt the same way.

"You're not wrong."

Ant savoured each of the threadbare components.

"Hard to imagine these cars are still made by hand, isn't it? I imagine some people have tried to persuade Morgan to automate production: you know, just in time, multiskilled assemblers and all that stuff."

Ant noticed Fitch rolling his eyes.

"What?"

He threw an oily rag across the exposed framework of the car.

Ant watched on as Fitch caught the stained fabric with a flourish of his hand.

"You sound like one of those consultants that steal your watch and sell you the time for six hundred quid a day. And here, you can have this back."

Tilting to the left, Ant dodged the blackened fabric, watching as it shot past and landed in a limp heap on the rough concrete floor.

"You know, like someone always banging on about forward planning and pressing the pedal to the metal. Now who might that be? Oh, I know. You!"

Ant smiled as his friend placed a finger to his lips, widening his eyes in fake surprise.

To a stranger, it might seem as though their verbal sparring could lead to fisticuffs.

Ant knew he could trust Fitch. They thrived on sharp banter, each calculated barb further reinforcing the already strong bond between them.

Ant was keen to change the subject now that he'd failed on the sarcasm front.

"Where's that half-inch spanner?"

Fitch obliged by gently throwing the tool, its trajectory aimed with care to force Ant into a full-stretch catch.

"Glad to see you still can still put your cricketing skills to good use."

Ant smiled before both men returned to their respective tasks, absorbed in the motoring history that lay before them.

Fitch was the first to break the silence.

"It'll be great to see her on the road again."

"You're right there, matey. A Morgan isn't something you see around here every day, is it?"

The mechanic nodded.

"Funny you should say that. There's a stranger running around the village in Morgan's latest Plus Six model. One of the Moonstone first editions. Must have cost him a packet. I tell you, he looked a right chav in his designer T-shirt and shades plonked on his head."

Ant's ears pricked up.

"Shades? This time of year? Bozo."

"Precisely, Ant. Seems he's intent on building some posh houses on that plot of land behind poor Ethan's place. It seems he can't develop the site without getting his hands on Glebe Cottage and demolishing it."

Looks like it's going to be a frosty one again, thought Lyn as she gazed at the jet-black sky and clear, full moon on her evening stroll around Stanton Parva.

She marvelled at the silhouetted rooftops of the higgledy-piggledy, thatched cottages.

I do love this place.

Lyn passed half a dozen teenagers pressed like sardines onto one of several wooden benches around the village green. She remembered doing the same thing on the same benches, only without the smartphones, when she was their age.

"Hi, miss," said one.

"Hi, Lyn," added a second, more confident girl.

She smiled. Lyn knew each of them. A few had siblings

at her school. Others because she'd taught them as a student teacher.

"Keep safe, you lot."

Lyn enjoyed the company of young people. She never ceased to be excited by even the small part she and her staff might play in helping them make the best of the opportunities that lie ahead of them. It was why she went into teaching and enjoyed watching young minds soak up new ideas and information.

I love it when kids think they are the first people in history to be their age, and only they can change the world.

None of the group responded. Instead, they smiled. Lyn sensed they had retreated back into their own world, from which adults were strictly excluded.

Not all Lyn's memories were pleasant ones as she skirted the village pond and looked over to a neat row of flint cottages.

Shoehorned between the butchers and the old post office, stood Lime View.

Lyn frowned as she remembered looking out of the window of her tiny bedroom as a nine-year-old. Downstairs, her parents would be quarrelling. It was usually about money or rather the lack of it. She'd hated having to tell the tally man *"Mum said can we leave it this week,"* and the angry look he'd give her.

At least I escaped to university.

A light breeze washed across Lyn's face as she rounded the corner into High Street and with it the seductive aroma of fried cod.

That sorts supper out.

Watching her step, Lyn navigated the raised threshold of Sid and Carol's fish and chip shop.

"Now then, stranger. We've not seen you in a while."

Sid spoke in his usual friendly tone. Lyn felt his jocular voice precisely fitted the rotund frame of a man in his late fifties too fond of his own cooking.

"It's only been two weeks, Sid. Glad to see you miss me."

They laughed as Carol walked through a connecting door holding a tray of fresh fish.

"Hi, Lyn. Who's a stranger, then?"

Her laid-back voice resonated around the white-tiled walls of the old shop.

Lyn smiled.

"Your husband thinks I'm neglecting you too."

She pointed a friendly finger towards Sid.

"Cod, chips, and mushy peas, please, Carol."

The slender woman looked at the empty, glass-fronted compartment above one of the fryers then at her husband in well-practised admonishment.

"Old fool," was all Carol had to say.

Lyn watched as Sid winked at her while taking the tray of fish from his wife.

"And remember, not too much beer batter this time."

Lyn looked on as Sid sighed and dipped the fish into the creamy mix before wiping the excess coating off, with an expert flick of his wrist against the side of the stainless-steel container. Finally, he lowered the cod into the bubbling oil between forefinger and thumb.

"Only twenty-two years I've been doing this, Lyn."

She held her arms up and stepped back from the counter as if in retreat.

"Don't involve me in your domestic tiffs."

"My darling husband, it's twenty-four years, if you must."

She turned to Lyn.

"Then again, he never remembers our anniversary either. I don't know why I bother."

Lyn directed a "tut tut" at Sid.

"I ask you, Lyn. What sort of husband gives his wife a birthday card for her wedding anniversary?"

Carol looked Sid full in the eye.

"If I were you, Sid, I'd be offering to make your wife a nice cup of tea."

Lyn could see Sid had clocked onto her strategy of side-stepping further embarrassment.

"Well, at least you get a card. I never get the same number of socks back that I put into the wash basket."

The two women laughed as the image of Sid walking around in odd socks sank into their collective consciousness.

"Fish will be out in a minute, Lyn," said Carol as she moved the cod around the fryer with a long-handled pan skimmer. "Awful what happened to Ethan, wasn't it?"

Lyn thought for a split second how she should answer. Perhaps Carol might have picked up something on the village grapevine that could prove useful.

"Yes, dreadful."

Lyn took note of Carol's reaction. The woman looked thoughtful as she gave the pan skimmer another swish around the fryer.

"And finding a new church warden won't be easy. Reverend Morton can be a funny devil when he wants."

Lyn raised an eyebrow. Carol let out a short, sharp laugh having realised she'd just compared a man of God with Satan.

Lyn continued with her cautious approach.

"I suppose we can all be a bit funny when the mood takes us, Carol."

The woman nodded as she busied herself wiping away

the excess oil from the edge of the fryer with a spotlessly clean cloth.

"That's true. But from what I saw the other day, those two weren't getting on."

Lyn's intrigue intensified as Carol continued.

"I was only saying to Sid this morning that I stumbled across them in the church going at it like two ferrets in a sack after evensong. Red in the face, both of them, they were."

I wonder what that could have been about?

Lyn frowned as she rested her elbows on the stainless-steel counter and leant forward.

"I see. I wonder what that could have been about?"

Lyn watched as Carol submerged the skimmer into the oil and lifted the newly fried cod into the heated storage shelf above.

"Sid thought it was something to do with the collection. Maybe the warden accused the vicar of pinching some of it."

Lyn shook her head in disbelief.

"Surely not. After all, he's the vicar!"

Carol mirrored Lyn's movement and leant forward, whispering so as not to be overheard.

"From what I could make out, Ethan told the vicar he would report him to—"

Carol suddenly straightened up and turned her attention to a new customer entering the shop.

"Mrs Oldsworth. Nice to see you again. You've come with the Girl Guides' order, have you?"

Lyn finished putting salt and vinegar on her supper, scooped up the tray, and after exchanging goodbyes, made her way to the door.

I need to talk to Ant about this.

4

SCHOOL DAYS

Ant smiled as Lyn's secretary closed the door behind him.

"You're lucky. She who must be obeyed is between meetings.

He knew what a good gatekeeper Tina was at keeping distraction away from Lyn and considered himself lucky to be granted an audience.

"How's your week been, then? Ant knew his enquiry would ensure he stayed in her good books.

"Oh, you know. Usual stuff, patching kids up, and keeping disgruntled parents away from Her Majesty." Tina pointed towards Lyn's office. "And it's Wednesday, so it's an evening at Cinema World in Norwich for me."

Ant warmed to the theme. "Anything good on?"

Tina's eyes lit up. "You betcha; it's only the director's cut of *The Thing from Another World*'. Speaking of which, I suppose I should announce your arrival."

"I've an odd-looking bloke wearing a scruffy, waxed, shooting jacket and mucky boots slouching in front of me, who insists he knows you. Should I send him on his way, or do you want to see him?"

The intercom clicked as Tina pressed the receive button.

A few seconds of silence followed, which Ant assumed was for dramatic effect.

"That'll be Ant, I suppose? Send him in, but tell him to wipe his feet first."

Ant knew Lyn's white painted office was immaculate. The sterile space always made him feel as if he were about to undergo root-canal treatment.

"The head will see you now."

Tina smiled.

Ant guessed she was enjoying the moment.

"Will she now?"

He raised an eyebrow and waited to be shown through.

"Oh, and I don't know why you bother with that inter-thingy. I could hear her through the door, you know."

Ant nodded his head toward Lyn's office.

"I heard that," said a voice from the other side of a half-glazed door.

Ant smiled at the secretary.

"I rest my case."

"Whatever," said Tina as she opened the connecting door, stood to one side, and allowed Ant to pass.

"Coffee?"

Lyn looked up from a heap of papers.

"I'll have my usual. The scruffy one will have an Americano with two sweeteners."

"Will I, indeed?"

Ant lifted a moulded steel chair from one side of the small room and sat opposite Lyn.

"You know you're not supposed to have sugar, so I'm looking out for you. That's what mates do, isn't it?"

His friend had too much of a twinkle in her eye for Ant's liking.

"You wouldn't believe how much paperwork there is in this job. Just look at it."

Lyn swept a hand across the desk to emphasise her point.

"This lot is just about health and safety. See that pile—finance stuff. And that," she said, pointing to a thick document, "is a Department for Education consultation, due in next week."

Ant sniffed and looked at a small rectangle landscape photo on one of the bare walls as if disinterested in his friend's woes.

"I wondered what you got up to all day. After all, it's only a tiny school, isn't it?"

He watched as Lyn's mouth opened and prepared himself for the onslaught.

"Sounds like you're both ready for a snack," said Tina as she entered the room and placed a tray holding two coffees and four chocolate digestive biscuits on the desk between the sparring partners.

Ant pointed at the biscuits.

"No added sugar, I hope?"

Tina wagged a finger as she retraced her steps to the door.

"Watch it, you."

The next few seconds passed in silence as the two mates savoured the coffee and dunked their respective digestive biscuits.

"So what have you been up to, Ant?"

She dipped the tip of her index finger into her mug to retrieve a small piece of her snack from the hot liquid.

Trying not to smirk, he watched Lyn wince in pain from

a scalded fingertip.

"You do that every time."

She savoured the piece of soggy digestive while shaking her hand as if to eject the pain from her pinked finger.

"Can't waste any, can I?"

Ant shook his head and smiled.

"To answer your question, I've been doing my Morgan up with Fitch and—"

"Boys and their toys, eh?"

As she spoke, Lyn peered into her coffee to ensure every morsel of the biscuit had been rescued.

"And we're making good progress replacing the wishbones—"

"Wishbones? Why are you putting bits of chicken into that silly car of yours?"

Ant gave Lyn the crushed look of a man having his most treasured possession trashed. He slouched into the angular frame of the uncomfortable metal chair, only to quickly sit up again due to a sudden pain in his coxis.

"Lynda Blackthorn, you know full well that a wishbone strut is part of the driving assembly of a car. You helped my father enough times when we were kids and know almost as much about Morgans as I do."

It was clear to Ant that Lyn intended to keep her council even though his use of her full name was meant to provoke. Her knowing smile displayed all he needed to know.

I'll get the better of you one day, thought Ant.

Lyn brushed a hand across the piles of paper again.

"Anyway, why are you here? I'm rather busy, you know."

Ant looked indignant.

"You were the one who said we needed to catch up. But if you don't want to know the stranger, that's all right. I'll follow up on the lead myself."

Ant knew the mention of a new lead would whet Lyn's curiosity.

He watched as she placed her coffee on the desk and looked at him expectantly.

"You mean you *do* think Ethan was murdered?"

"Well, let's not get ahead of ourselves, but Fitch told me about a property developer who's been sniffing around the village. Apparently, he wants to build a dozen or so 'executive' houses on the field behind Glebe Cottage."

Lyn returned her second biscuit to the plate instead of dunking it.

"But what has that got to do with Ethan?"

Ant lifted a blank piece of paper from the edge of Lyn's desk and picked up one of several coloured pens scattered across the desktop.

He drew a rough sketch of the field, Glebe Cottage, and the main road in front of the house.

"Do you see? That developer can't build without owning Ethan's place and knocking it down. It's the only access from the road onto the field. Without Ethan's place, that development will not happen."

Lyn's eyes widened as the details sank in.

"So you're saying that one way or another the stranger with the posh car needed Ethan out of the way?"

"Got it in one."

Ant scrunched the scrap of paper, taking careful aim, then lobbed it with the deftest of touches into an empty wastepaper basket.

"Hole in one."

Irritated at Lyn's lack of interest in his party trick, Ant watched as she sat back in her leather swivel chair, swinging it from side to side.

"Well, Anthony, you're not the only one with a scoop."

Ant involuntarily raised both eyebrows as he reacted to the increasing excitement with which Lyn spoke.

"I was in the chip shop last night and—"

Lyn's train of thought evaporated as the door opened.

"Your eleven o'clock is here," said Tina with just the upper part of her body appearing around the door. Ant realised that her facial expression made it clear that II a.m. meant II a.m.

"Tell you what, Lyn. Why don't we catch up in the Wherry Arms tonight? In the meantime, there's something I want to check out anyway."

Ant watch Lyn as she prised herself from the chair and smoothed the fabric of her pencil skirt and jacket.

He was impressed with her sudden switch to head teacher mode in preparation for whatever her meeting involved.

"That's fine, Ant. See you tonight."

He could see she was already mentally in another place.

Leaving Tina's outer office, Ant glimpsed an agitated woman, her glare fixed on Lyn.

Glad I don't have to deal with parents looking to punch my lights out, he thought.

THE WHERRY ARMS was quiet for a Wednesday evening as Ant and Lyn settled into the tiny snug of the ancient hostelry.

"Well," said Ant as the pair sat around a small, circular table. "Ethan did not commit suicide: no doubt in my mind now."

He watched as Lyn took a sip of her lemonade spritzer, her eyes now fixed on his.

"You had some doubt, then?"

Ant savoured his pint of Fen Bodger pale ale.

"I know Riley insisting it was suicide is enough to think the opposite, but I wanted to be sure. Well, now that I've seen the autopsy photographs, I'm certain."

Lyn almost choked on her drink.

"You've seen what? How on earth—"

"Told you before, Lyn," said Ant, interjecting, "the job I do, or should I now say, did, has its perks. Turns out the pathologist is an old mucker of mine from the army. We worked together on..."

Ant's words faded as he recalled the circumstances of their previous cooperation while on active duty.

He gazed into his pint glass watching the bubbles making their way to the surface. He knew Lyn had cottoned on. He found her awareness reassuring.

"Come on, Ant. Snap out of it. Tell me about the photos."

Ant reacted positively to Lyn's abrupt approach. It worked, though he knew he would need help sooner rather than later.

"There were two rope burns around Ethan's neck. It took some finding, but there's a distinct, but narrow line of bruising buried beneath the rope used in Stanton Woods. It looks as though—"

"Wait a minute. Are you saying someone strangled Ethan, and he was..." interrupted Lyn.

Ant saw the look of disgust spreading across her face as she struggled to complete the sentence.

"Still alive when he was strung up?"

He reached over the table and cupped Lyn's hand.

"I'm afraid it's quite likely, Lyn. If there's one saving

grace, he'd have been unconscious, if not already dead, by the time he was strung up, poor chap."

Ant loosened his hold on Lyn's hand and instead gently stroked the freckled skin to give some reassurance.

"The thing is, Ant, if that developer bloke *was* involved, I don't think he was working alone."

Ant frowned.

"What brings you to that conclusion?"

Lyn swilled the remains of her drink around the tall glass in a slow, circular motion.

"I don't want two and two to make five, but remember this morning when I started to tell you about the fish and chip shop?"

Lyn retold the conversation she'd had with Carol.

"And that was on Sunday, the day before Sally and Jessica found Ethan."

Ant watch Lyn as she took a final swig of her drink, emptying its contents in one go and placed the now empty glass back onto the table, rotating it between her hands.

He followed suit by tipping his glass at a sharp angle and demolishing the final third of his pint.

"Okay, this is what we'll do," said Ant as he gathered the two glasses and got to his feet. "I'll track down the developer. Can you sound out the vicar without tipping him off to what we're up to?"

"Love to. The only thing is, I'm covering for a sick colleague tomorrow, so it's fractions and spelling with year four all day for me—yuck!"

Ant smiled. He suspected her pupils hated that stuff as much as he had.

"No worries," replied Ant. "I'll sort it, and let you know how I got on."

5

MORNING PRAYERS

T hursday morning broke with a clear blue sky, which framed a corn-yellow sun in all its late autumn glory.

What a great place to live, thought Ant as he walked the two miles from Stanton Hall to the village. He scanned an uninterrupted view of Stanton Broad and its floodplain. The ancient landscape was so different from the manicured gardens and open parkland of the Hall but no less breathtaking.

Ant glimpsed a wherry moving serenely along the Broad and figured the owners were taking a late season holiday.

The skipper's doing well to catch what little wind there is, he thought as he watched in wonderment while the triangular sail rippled in the light breeze.

Within twenty minutes, he was on the outskirts of the village: his gaze once more drawn to the church.

This is the second time in two days I've sensed the need to go inside. What's going on?

He entered the already open door and slipped silently onto the pew nearest the exit. He watched Reverend Morton look down the nave of the church. Ant assumed the six other parishioners were regulars for the morning service. None of them, it seemed to Ant, were under seventy.

"Just a few announcements before I finish."

Ant watched as the vicar's scattered audience began to fidget.

Perhaps they're competing to be first out the door.

Lyn had mentioned to Ant that the vicar had a reputation for roping the unwary into some "voluntary" task or other as he shook their hand at the end of the service and wished them a good day.

"We have just said prayers for the soul of our dear brother Ethan. To celebrate his life, I wish to announce this morning that we will be holding a special service of thanksgiving. It will take place a week on Sunday. I ask you all to spread the word so that as many villagers as possible have an opportunity to join us."

Ant watched as the proposition was met with general approval, apart from Phyllis and therefore Betty. He surmised the pair positioned themselves towards the rear of the church to better see who was in the church, who was sitting next to whom, and if any salacious gossip was to be had.

I bet they beat the vicar to the door to escape getting roped into anything.

Busy criticising the poor show of flowers, the two women prattled away to each other. Ant guessed they heard little of what the reverend had to say.

"Gladys Bircham never was any good at flower arranging," said Phyllis. She pointed to a dismal display of hellebores drooping from a vase next to the pulpit. "Remember at school when she brought that deadly nightshade in and almost killed us?"

Ant knew that Betty may have wished to respond but

realized there was little point since Phyllis would only cut her off midflow.

"Nineteen thirty-eight, that was," continued Phyllis, "and what did she end up as? A flaming nurse. I ask you."

Ant watched Betty bristle at the use of intemperate language in church. He knew what the problem was: she lacked the courage to rebuke her lifelong friend.

"Have you a question, Mrs Plumstead, or are we just gossiping?" asked the vicar.

Ever the diplomat, Reverend, thought Ant.

His question threw Phyllis off guard. It had been so long since anyone in the village had used her married name. Although Archie had died over two decades earlier, she still missed his quiet contentedness, particularly his habit of coming home from work and dozing in front of the fire each night after tea until bedtime.

"Me, Reverend? What makes you think I have anything to say?"

Ant smiled as Betty looked at the floor and pinched her little nose in, which he assumed was a well-practised routine to stop herself giggling. He could see that the remaining parishioners felt no such need for restraint.

The more agitated Phyllis became watching several sets of shoulders rising and falling in unison, the more amusing Ant thought the scene.

Ant gave credit to the vicar for having made his point not pursuing the matter further.

I imagine he's ready for his coffee and a tot of brandy.

"Go in peace," added the reverend after leading his congregation in a final prayer.

Within seconds, he disappeared into the vestry. Ant knew the clergyman needed to make a quick dash around the outside of the church to appear at the entrance and catch his parishioners on their way out.

Although Ant was nearest the door, he waited until everyone else had left, nodding to each as they passed in turn.

Things didn't quite go as Ant had planned. As he exited the church, he saw that the vicar was deep in conversation with a parishioner.

It was plain to Ant that the reverend was eager to evade the woman's clutches, and from the bit of conversation he could overhear, avoid what seemed to be a regular invitation to Sunday lunch.

As Ant drew nearer and caught the vicar's eye, the reverend seemed to grasp his opportunity.

"Ah, there you are, Anthony. Mrs Redwood, thank you so much for your kind offer, but there is a matter on which I must speak to this gentleman."

Ant couldn't help but notice the forlorn body language the woman had adopted. She passed by with a look that left little to Ant's imagination.

"Oh dear," said Ant as he acknowledged the vicar's awkward smile.

"It's uncharitable of me to say, I know, but you've saved my digestive system from a dreadful fate. Still, I'm glad you've called by. I wanted to thank you for your wonderful contribution to the church bell restoration fund. Such an important cause, and your family are, as always, such generous benefactors."

The compliment threw Ant.

I guess Dad must have signed the cheque.

"Think nothing of it."

He tried to hide his ignorance of the matter.

"The village owes such a lot to the church, and by extension, to you."

Ant was pleased that it was now the vicar's turn to blush.

"Not at all," replied the reverend.

"It was a good service. Very thoughtful subject matter today."

Ant watched as the clergyman frowned and raised his arms outwards before allowing them to free fall back to his sides with a thud.

"Yes, but God's words touch fewer and fewer people as each season passes. What to do? That's the question. What to do?"

Ant was keen to probe the vicar about Ethan. He still had his reservations, despite his military training, to exclude no possibility, no matter how fantastic, from any investigation. But could the clergyman really have been involved in the man's murder?

He turned to look across the graveyard that surrounded the church. An imperfect pattern of headstones tilting at crazy angles gave testament to a thousand years of sacred history.

"Not to put too fine a point on it, Vicar. You now have one less parishioner."

Let's see where this takes us, he thought.

The vicar bridled at Ant's sudden mention of the late church warden. Ant knew he'd hit a nerve but wasn't sure if it was genuine remorse he was observing or an involuntary defensive reaction.

"Very sad. Such a gentle-mannered man. Never a bad word to say about anyone. Do you know, Anthony, I don't think I ever heard Ethan raise his voice in all the time I knew him."

Time to push. That's not what Carol said she'd seen.

"Except with you, Reverend." Ant fixed his gaze on the man.

Ant noticed the clergyman stiffen.

"What do you mean, Anthony? My relationship with Ethan was always cordial. The only—"

He hesitated.

"But you *did* argue with Ethan recently, didn't you?"

The reverend's eyes began to glisten with tears.

Is this about regret at being rumbled, or grief?

"It's true. We did argue. And now he's dead. Lord forgive me."

Ant moderated his tone. He saw the effect of whatever had happened between the two men take hold in the vicar's mind.

"About those falling congregations, Anthony. That also means less money from collections and bequests. The archbishop has threatened to close St Mary's if things don't improve."

Ant was not a religious man, but the thought of a place of worship his family had been involved with for generations ceasing to exist appalled him.

Can't let that happen.

"But what's that got to do with Ethan, Vicar?"

Ant observed the man's body language as he retrieved a pristine, white handkerchief from his vestment. The reverend carefully unfolded the material before cupping it around his nose for a second or two.

"I wanted to remove the pews so that we could use the space more flexibly. You know the sort of thing. Hiring the church out for events and suchlike."

"Sounds a logical approach to try."

"I thought so too, Anthony. But Ethan..."

Ant sensed the vicar hesitating as his emotions got the

better of him.

"Ethan opposed the move. He said it was going against the Christian tradition and would have none of it."

Ant allowed Reverend Morton to compose himself before pressing the point.

"Could he have stopped you?"

The vicar shook his head.

"No, but he could have made things very difficult. He was so well respected in the village. Do you know that pews were only used on a regular basis in English churches after the Reformation? I told him that, but he wouldn't listen. Instead he threatened to get up a petition."

Ant shrugged his shoulders.

"But, Vicar, you could just have told the villagers about the archbishop's threat."

"That's the point, Anthony. The archbishop forbade me to say anything to anyone until he'd made a final decision. What was I to do?"

The vicar's dilemma caught Ant off guard. Did he just happen to be a man in the wrong place at the wrong time when he was overheard by Carol? On the other hand, he had a motive and the opportunity to murder Ethan. But was he a killer? And how could he have strung the man up?

Stranger things have happened, thought Ant.

The vicar looked at his inquisitor with alarm.

"You don't think I killed Ethan, do you? For goodness' sake, Anthony."

His voice began to break.

Not the time to ease off.

"It doesn't matter what I do or don't believe, Vicar. It just doesn't look good, does it? When Detective Inspector Riley gets hold of you, he'll think it's Christmas."

Ant sensed the vicar beginning to panic.

"Don't worry, he doesn't know about you arguing with Ethan. At least not yet. But I need your help. Was there anything else bothering the warden?"

He could see the relief washing over the vicar's face.

"Anything at all, Vicar?"

"Ethan hadn't been himself for weeks. I'm sure that's why he argued with me. It just wasn't like him."

Ant placed a hand on the vicar's lower arm.

"What do you think was going on?"

The clergyman's eyes flickered as if processing a Rolodex for information.

"He was such a private man, Anthony. But there was one thing he said some weeks ago. Now I come to think about it, his mood changed around that time."

"Go on," urged Ant.

"Grindle. His name was Grindle. Something about land. But it didn't make any sense to me."

It does to me, thought Ant.

6

THE BUTTERCROSS

"What are you looking so flustered about?"

"Flustered? You know I have to be back at school for a governor's meeting within the hour. What kept you? I've got you a bacon bap from the tearoom. Might just about still be warm."

Ant smiled expectantly as he retrieved a crumpled, brown paper bag containing his lunch from Lyn's outstretched hand. His nostrils flared as the warming aroma of the honey-roast snack wafted over him.

"Did you remember to get brown sauce?" asked Ant as he peered into the simple packaging.

"Don't push it. Lord or not, you can like it or lump it."

Ant stretched to catch a paper napkin Lyn had thrown in his general direction. The shot fell just short so that Ant was forced to bend down in order to retrieve it.

"I take it that bowing before the school head teacher is my penance for getting above myself?"

He saw immediately that his tongue-in-cheek remark had failed to cut it with Lyn. Ant winced at being on the receiving end of her harshest head-teacher stare, gesturing with a crooked finger for him to join her on the buttercross steps.

"Why are we eating out in the cold when there's plenty of room in the tearoom?"

He pointed at the near empty establishment on the opposite side of the street. Ant's enquiry met with indifference.

"Never mind that; anyway, fresh air is good for you. Now how did you get on with the vicar?"

His expression exposed his disagreement with Lyn's view on the efficaciousness of the chilled environment. And he wasn't just thinking about the weather.

Fresh air, indeed. It's starting to flaming snow.

Accepting Lyn had refused his plea for a cosy chair by the open fire in Dotti's Coffee and Book Emporium, he recounted his meeting with Reverend Morton.

"I suppose you could say his explanation for the fallout with Ethan is plausible, but—"

Ant wasn't best pleased to be cut off midsentence.

"Oh dear. I think we're about to get the third degree." Ant's eyeline followed Lyn's index finger in the direction of a police Jaguar. The car's deceleration and blinking left indicator confirmed their worst fears.

"He's clocked us, Lyn. If we'd have eaten in the damned tearoom, Inspector Plod wouldn't have seen us. And I haven't even finished my bacon bap."

The pair watched as Riley rolled out of the police car and strode towards them, a finger pointing for added dramatic effect.

"I told you two to keep your noses out of this case, didn't I?"

"He's not happy, is he?" muttered Ant to Lyn as he scoffed

down the last of his snack, spraying bits of bread on Lyn's coat in his haste not to be cheated out of lunch.

He watched as Lyn shot him an icy stare and brushed the lapel of her coat.

"Do you mind, you mucky pup?"

Ant shrugged his shoulders and offered a weak smile like a naughty boy caught scrumping.

Ant, concluding that discretion was the better form of valour, averted his gaze, and instead, concentrated on the pathetic figure of the detective now standing a few feet away.

"You look a little flushed, Inspector. Do you have a problem with blood pressure?"

Ant adopted his most assertive pose as he awaited an answer and watched a white skull cap form over the policeman's thinning hair.

"Do come under the canopy; all that snow on your head cannot be good for either your blood pressure or follicles, although I have read some scientific evidence that intense cold can stimulate hair growth. What do you think, Inspector?"

Ant's tone of faux concern served only to enrage the already agitated policeman.

Ant noticed that although it was Riley's choice to close the gap between them, he appeared intensely uncomfortable being so near another human being.

"I neither have a problem with blood pressure nor thinning hair." Riley hesitated for a second or two before continuing. "Anyway, so-called 'cold therapy' doesn't work. In fact, it just gives you a headache."

Ant almost choked on the last crumbs of his bap as he watched Riley blush all the more as it dawned he'd confirmed having the very problem he'd just denied.

Ant could hear Lyn chortling behind him. He nudged her arm by way of telling her to stop.

He felt her lean into him.

"That hurt," was all he heard before he felt himself being propelled into Riley.

Ant was unsure who now felt the most uncomfortable as the two men disentangled from each other, each giving a manly grunt and looking at the snow-covered ground.

Ant threw Lyn a scowl then turned back to Riley and observed displaced ice from the policeman's scalp slithering down the detective's purple cheeks.

"Would you like a tissue, Detective Inspector? That must be uncomfortable," said Lyn. She stretched her right hand out, a paper napkin pinched between two fingers. "It's only got a little bacon fat on it, but I'm sure it'll do the job just fine."

Ant watched Riley snarl but grudgingly hold out his hand to accept Lyn's gift. That was until mention of the bacon fat.

Not as daft as I thought, mused Ant.

"Thank you, but no," replied Riley, stiffening his gait. "You may think us stupid in tolerating meddlesome members of the public, such as yourselves. This does not mean, however, that our patience is without limit."

Ant noted the growl with which the detective spat his words and considered the man had decided that attack was the better form of defence.

"You spoke to my pathologist, didn't you?" said Riley.

Ant gave the man a look of disdain.

"Do you own him, then?"

His response left no room for confusion about his dislike of the policeman.

"I thought the days of serfdom in this country had long gone?"

Ant could see Riley was unsure how to respond. Here was a member of the aristocracy lecturing him about serfdom. What to do?

Eventually, the silence was broken.

"You would know more about such matters than me, Lord Stanton."

Ant smirked, allowing the detective to think he'd put him back in some imaginary box, however, and semblance of reasserted authority vanished from Riley as the last remains of snow on his scalp started to move. The white carpet slid past the detective's left ear and hit the floor with the dull thud of a snowball hitting its target.

"There, now. That must feel better," quipped Lyn.

"Hope you don't feel too light-headed," added Ant.

Denying Riley time to respond, Ant pressed on.

"Oh, we did away with all that serf stuff in 2010. We all have to change our ways, Detective Inspector. You know, a bit like the police not being on the take these days. Or perhaps some are. What do you think?"

He watched as Riley's eyes narrowed. Ant had done his homework and knew suspicion had followed the detective for years. The force's response was to move him around the country.

Out of sight, out of mind, eh?

"And how are you liking Norfolk? Where was it you served previously? And before that?" It was not a question to which Ant expected an answer. He'd made his point. Riley's reaction confirmed as much.

"Anyway, you were talking about the pathologist. You know, the one it seems you own? Well, you may wish to know Quentin and I served Queen and Country together. I heard on the grapevine that he was working in Norwich, so I toddled off to the big city and said my hellos. Nothing wrong with that, is there?"

Ant sensed Riley had become distracted.

"Are you listening, Detective Inspector?"

Fed up with having a damp scalp, Riley produced a crumpled tissue from his coat pocket and dabbed his fore-head. Ant guessed it gave him a chance to think of a response to his deliberate baiting.

"I've told you both. Ethan Baldwin committed suicide. There are no suspicious circumstances. No mysterious cult hanging people by the full moon. No celestial beings venting a vengeance from heaven on one of their own."

Ant cut Riley's self-congratulatory response short.

"Careful, Inspector. That's blasphemy and is absolutely uncalled for."

Ant knew his riposte would unnerve the detective. After all, how was he to know the son of an earl didn't have connections in the church or wider establishment that had the power to harm his career?

Satisfied his ploy had worked, judging by Riley's slumped shoulder, Ant went in for the kill.

"Anyway, Detective, let's not get bogged down in theology, and of course you'll know all about the tiff between Ethan Baldwin and the vicar, won't you?"

Ant's tone was measured in the extreme.

He watched the detective.

"Never mind what I do, or do not, know about the vicar and Mr Baldwin."

Well done, Detective. You didn't fall for that one.

"Let this be a final warning. If either of you get in my way again, I'll nick you. Do you understand?"

Ant turned to Lyn as the detective retraced his steps to

the Jaguar.

"That was fun."

"Anthony, you are a tease, and you'll come undone one of these days, young man. Anyway, do you think he knows?"

Ant laughed and pulled Lyn by the hand as they walked gingerly across the ice-covered cobblestones towards Dotti's place.

"You bet he knows. It was written all over his face. Look."

Ant pointed at the Jaguar roaring out of the village with an icy spray spitting from its rear wheels.

"He's heading for the vicarage."

"Never mind the car. You'll go too far with him one of these days. Like it or not, he can make both our lives a misery if he wishes to."

Ant didn't react. Instead, he looked into the now empty paper bag which had contained his lunch, blew into it, and scrunched it closed. With a swift thump with his free hand he exploded it, which resulted in an almighty bang.

He watched Lyn, who had been looking the other way, jump with shock.

"You always do that, fool."

He could see she was far from pleased.

Ant's schoolboy smirk signalled his contentedness with recent events.

"His chief inspector knows Riley's an idiot. He doesn't want him here anymore than we do."

Lyn snatched what remained of the paper bag.

"And you know this for a fact, do you?"

Ant's smile broadened.

"You might say so. I couldn't possible comment."

His tone was meant to intrigue.

Lyn busied herself picking bits of bap from Ant's collar. He made no attempt to stop her.

"So why did you tell Riley about the vicar? Haven't you just dropped him in it?"

Ant shook his head.

"As I said, he must have suspected him already. I just wanted him to know that we knew, to wind him up. If the vicar *is* up to something, Riley will frighten him to death, which may flush the man out for us."

Ant brushed a thin layer of snow from Lyn's shoulder.

"So you think it's worth keeping our eye on Reverend Morton?"

Ant nodded.

"As we've both admitted, he has a plausible explanation for the argument with Ethan. Nevertheless, I sense there's something going on in the background he doesn't want anyone to know about. Let's hope it's not covering the tracks of a murder."

He watched as Lyn's mood darkened. He could have kicked himself for overlooking the obvious.

Mustn't forget how close Lyn is to the church.

"Enough of the sad face," said Ant, keen to lift his friend's mood. "Are you still in touch with that old boyfriend of yours? You know, the one in the planning department in Cromer?"

He watched as Lyn gave him a world weary sort of look.

"You know quite well I see him from time to time, so don't be so obvious. What do you want me to do?"

Ant pulled ahead of Lyn, keen to reach the coffee shop as sanctuary against the worsening weather.

"Oh, just wondered if you might ask your sweetheart a question or two, strictly for the good of our investigations, you understand."

Ant got no more than five paces before Lyn's well-aimed snowball caught his exposed neck.

7

PAPER TRAIL

F riday morning prayers progressed in their usual efficient way. Today, like every day, Reverend Morton led his dwindling flock in contemplation and thanks.

Except today it was a troubled vicar who trudged back to the vestry.

He stowed the medieval chalice and silver plate back into the safe before undoing and hanging up his vestments. The vicar then slumped into a simple wooden chair, which fitted to perfection in its frugal surroundings.

It took less than a minute to count the collection and enter the total in the church ledger.

The archbishop's words swirled around his head.

"Sort the finances out, or I'll deconsecrate the church."

He thought his superior's words harsh for a senior cleric.

Whatever happened to charity? reflected the vicar.

The stillness allowing the vicar to ponder his dilemma did not last long. His mobile started to dance across the table, its screen illuminated with a name he knew well.

Swiping the screen to the right with his thumb, the vicar heard a familiar voice.

"Yes, I know we agreed," he responded. "There's something I must do first. I'll be with you as soon as I can."

Reverend Morton didn't wait for a response. Instead, he ended the call and slid the phone into the inside pocket of his jacket.

Locking the vestry door, the vicar walked to the front entrance of the church. He then turned left to walk through the old graveyard. Staring at one grave after another, he kept seeing the same surnames crop up. He was aware some locals were able to trace their families back hundreds of years.

I just can't allow this sacred place to close.

In the near distance he saw Glebe Cottage, its name picked out in white lettering on a piece of carved wood fixed to the ornate wrought-iron front gate.

Reverend Morton reflected on what "Glebe" stood for. It meant a cottage, and the land the building stood on had once belonged to the church.

If only we still owned it, the church's financial future would be secure.

Seconds later, he stood at the back door of Ethan's home. It had been unoccupied for just a few days. Already it looked forlorn waiting for its owner to return.

The vicar looked over his shoulder checking to see if anyone was about.

Soon he concentrated his gaze to a small, glazed earthenware planter by the door. It had been there for as long as he could remember. Stooping down he tipped it on its edge and retrieved a key. He'd warned Ethan many times not to leave it under the jar. Now he was glad the warden had failed to heed his advice.

Crossing the kitchen, he made his way into the hallway; the vicar took care not to touch any surfaces. A pair of delicate, white gloves he used for polishing the church silver served their purpose as he turned a Victorian brass doorknob.

The vicar was keen no one should know, at least not the police, that he'd been in the cottage.

As he entered the front room, he felt as if Ethan had just nipped out to collect his morning paper and would be back at any moment. On the dining table rested a half-drunk cup of tea. In the saucer, the remains of a wafer biscuit.

Reverend Morton tried hard not to notice the ordinariness of it all.

He shuffled through the tidy row of lever-box files that lined an alcove next to the chimney breast. He opened one then another as he searched in vain for the vital document.

His frustration surfaced as he thumbed the final cardboard container. The vicar prised back the sprung plastic arm that held its contents secure with so much force that it snapped into several pieces, each fragment flying in a different direction.

Convinced his mission had been a failure, he turned and made his way back towards the door. In doing so, he knocked a crossword puzzle book from the arm of Ethan's favourite chair. Bending down to retrieve the publication, he noticed a sheaf of paper nestled between its pages.

"Thank the Lord." Such was the relief that he couldn't help speaking out loud to an empty house.

The vicar leafed through the pages held together at one corner with a paper clip.

He had found what he'd been looking for.

As the adrenalin rush subsided, he became increasingly aware of the precarious position he now found himself in.

How would he explain being in Ethan's cottage?

In his haste to exit the building, he decided to save a few

seconds and leave by the front door instead of his planned route to keep out of sight via the back door and through Ethan's vegetable garden to the church.

It was a mistake.

"Good morning, Vicar," quipped a relaxed voice.

Reverend Morton looked up from the stone paving slabs, with a start. He hadn't expected to come across anyone.

"Ah, er, Tina. How are you this morning?"

In his agitated state, the words tumbled over one another.

He watched in terror as the school secretary smiled.

"Thank you, I'm—"

"Good, good," he said, not waiting for Tina to finish. "Can't stop. God's work will not wait." As he spoke, he pushed the sheaf of papers into his cassock.

"So, at the moment, Anthony, there's not too much to worry about."

Ant was thankful for the reassurance as he showed Dr Thorndike into the library of Stanton Hall. A thermos flask of coffee rested on a small table just inside the wide double doors of the exquisite book-lined room.

"Please, do take a seat. Coffee?"

Ant pointed to a leather carver to one side of the roaring fire.

"Just the job for this snowy weather. I suppose logs are something you have plenty of."

Ant watched as the doctor dropped into the deep pocketed, leather seat and leant forward, rubbing his hands together before the yellow-and-blue flames, licking the soot-covered, iron fireback.

"You should see what the garage is charging for a bag of logs these days."

Ant's face began to flush.

"It bears no relation to what we sell them to the garage for, I can tell you," replied Ant as he handed a steaming cup of coffee to the medic.

He noticed the doctor's amused look.

"Ah, I see. So you supply—"

Ant returned the physician's smile.

The two men spent the next few minutes exchanging views on the long-range forecast for the winter and amazement at how early in the season snow had fallen. All too soon the doctor returned to the subject of Ant's parents' health.

"As I said earlier, there is no immediate danger. However, heart failure is a debilitating condition. While your father is currently the stronger of the two, we should take nothing for granted."

Ant now understood that the doctor's lighthearted banter was his way of preparing the recipient to receive news of something less palatable.

Ant's background meant he wanted to get on with things.

I can deal with things I know about.

"Your prognosis?"

Ant couldn't take his eyes off the doctor as he once more turned to the roaring fire.

Let's have it, Doc.

"This cold spell will do your parents no good, whatsoever, so it's important that your father isn't allowed to gallivant around the estate."

Ant gazed into the remnants of his coffee.

"You know Dad as well as me, so fat chance of keeping him indoors."

Dr Thorndike rose from his chair.

"Yes, I know. But there is no option if we are to keep him with us for the longest time."

The words struck Ant like a thump to the head. He knew the reality of the situation. He just didn't want to hear the words.

"I suggest we occupy your father by getting him to tend your mother. You know, reading to her and so forth."

Ant looked up at the doctor and let out a throaty laugh.

"What? They'd kill one another. Mum's worse than Dad is when it comes to being nursed. You know how independent they both are."

The doctor nodded.

"I do, Anthony. But you should know this. If you fail to slow your father down, he may not live to see the summer. On the other hand, if he behaves, well—"

Ant shook his head, the small movement almost undetectable. He acknowledged that Thorndike had no need to finish his sentence.

"Not sure Dad has ever looked at life in those terms, Doctor. I'm certain he's not going to do so now."

The two men shared a look without the need to discuss the matter further. However, Ant sensed Thorndike wanted to ask him something. He guessed what was coming.

He felt the doctor's right hand coming to a gentle rest on his shoulder.

"And how are you doing, Anthony?"

Ant didn't react to the physical contact nor did he meet the doctor's concerned stare.

"You've heard, then?"

"Your father told me. He—"

"Dad? He doesn't know."

"I can assure you he does, Anthony. I doubt you're the only one who has military contacts, eh?"

The implications of the revelation appalled Ant. He'd wanted to keep it from his father until he felt ready to talk about it.

"You know your father. He's old school. He'll wait until you're ready to tell him. But there are two things I want you to bear in mind."

Thorndike had Ant's full attention.

"Your father cannot wait too much longer for you to say something."

Ant's eyes glistened as the doctor's words sank in.

"And you will pay a high price if you delay treatment for your PTSD for very long. But you know that already, don't you?"

Ant felt the doctor's gentle touch morph to a tight grip and immediately understood.

Delay on either front was not an option.

Ant nodded.

"I'll sort it, Doctor. And thank you. I guess I needed to hear that."

Ant nodded as he met the doctor's steely, but reassuring, look.

"Good. I'm here to help when you're ready. Speaking of which, I understand you've got together with Lyn again, so to speak?"

Ant bristled at the comment, though he didn't understand why.

"Well, I wouldn't say—"

"Doesn't matter on what basis you're seeing her, Anthony. Don't underestimate just how important it is to have someone you can trust to turn to. Do you understand?"

Ant had no need to reply. The look between them was enough.

"Anyway. I'll say goodnight."

The doctor slipped on his overcoat as Ant showed his visitor back into the cavernous hallway and opened the heavy entrance doors to the hall.

"Drive with care," shouted Ant as the doctor crossed a patch of snow-covered gravel towards his car.

"I will. With luck, the vicar is off the road now. The blighter almost killed me on my way over. He was driving like a madman. In a hurry to get somewhere by the looks of things."

8

THE OPEN ROAD

"I thought you said this thing was, how did you put it, 'in fine fettle.' It sounds ready for the scrapyard to me."

Lyn's words stung as Ant worked hard to keep the Morgan going despite the engine misfiring.

He was still feeling down after Dr Thorndike's visit. To top it all, his beloved Morgan began to misfire.

"I'll pull over to check. I'm certain it's nothing serious."

He could see Lyn looked far from convinced as he coaxed the stuttering car into a paddock at the top of a small rise. The sorry state of the Morgan was at odds with the stunning view over Stanton Parva.

"Well, it sounds serious to me, Ant."

Certain the engine was about to fail, Ant turned the engine off and glided the vehicle to a silent stop. Ratcheting the handbrake as far up as he could pull it, Ant depressed the clutch and put the car into first gear.

"You always do that. You know you're not supposed to leave a parked car in gear."

Ant chose to ignore his friend's criticism.

"Oh, I forgot. Since it's broken down, the car isn't going

anywhere, is it?" added Lyn. Her inflection delivered a with-
ering verdict.

Ant removed his back-to-front peaked cap and unfurled
a thick wool scarf from around his neck.

"And as I tell you every time, that's the way Dad taught
me to drive. Funnily enough, I haven't had a parked car run
away on me yet. Unlike someone I could mention."

Ant gave Lyn a knowing look.

"You know full well the handbrake was faulty that day.
The garage said so. Anyway, nobody got hurt."

He enjoyed the sight of Lyn in full displacement mode,
removing her wool bobble hat and undoing the zipper on
her winter coat for no particular reason other than to not
look at him.

Ant let out a belly laugh.

"That's if you don't include Arkwright's vegetable display
stand. Not to mention the squashed tomatoes. Looked like
the scene from *Apocalypse Now.*"

The more Ant laughed, the more annoyed he knew Lyn
was becoming. He also knew his friend would bide her time
since she clearly wasn't retaliating. Ant was the first to
acknowledge Lyn had the measure of him since they were at
school together as children.

Silence fell as the two friends took in their surroundings.
Having the soft top of the Morgan stowed away meant they
were able to take in the Norfolk night sky in all its majesty.

"Strange old world, Ant. "No matter what mess we cause
down here, everything up there seems to remain the same."

Even though Ant wanted to scrutinise the Morgan's
instrument display for an explanation of the car's bad
behaviour, he matched Lyn's gaze scanning a thousand
shimmering stars.

"I guess you're thinking about Ethan too, Ant?"

He looked across at her.

"Yes, I am."

"Have we got it all wrong? Could he have killed himself?"

Ant shook his head.

"We both know he didn't commit suicide. Let's think about what we *do* know. He was too frail to have got himself off the ground. Then there's the argument we know he had with the vicar."

He watched as Lyn's eyes widened. She was suddenly animated.

"Speaking about the vicar. I think your idea of using that daft detective to flush him out may have worked."

Ant's curiosity went into overdrive.

"What do you mean?"

"Well, Tina saw him coming out of Glebe Cottage. She said he looked as if he were trying to hide something from her. When she tried to engage him in conversation, he did a flit, pronto. Strange behaviour for a man of the cloth, don't you think?"

Ant nodded.

"More than strange because the doctor told me the vicar almost ran him off the road: said he was driving like a madman."

"Thorndike. Why have you been speaking to him?"

Oh dear. Now I've put my foot in it, thought Ant as he picked up on her concerned glance.

He reacted quickly to divert Lyn's line of questioning.

Not ready to discuss the topic yet.

"Er, what? Oh, I'll tell you later."

Ant took the opportunity to escape further questioning by opening the driver's door and climbing out.

"Strange name for a cottage, 'Glebe,' don't you think?"

As he spoke, Ant undid a leather strap holding the bonnet in place then lifted the cover to expose the full glory of the machine's engine.

"And I thought you liked history," responded Lyn as Ant's head disappeared into the engine compartment.

Thank heavens Lyn's not pushing the Thorndike thing.

Ant knew Lyn well enough to tell his reaction to the revelation was enough to stop further discussion on the matter: for the present, at any rate.

"Glebe refers to land owned by the church, Ant. Back in the day, the vicar was able to get an income from it to supplement his stipend from the church diocese."

Ant lifted his head from the engine, catching it on the bonnet as he did so. Massaging his scalp by way of checking for blood, he straightened himself and turned to Lyn.

"Who's been swallowing a dictionary, then?" Ant made no attempt to hide his sarcasm, although he could see it had no effect on Lyn.

"I did some village history with the kids a few weeks ago. One of the children asked about it, so I researched the subject. You know, like teachers do."

Now who's being sarcastic.

"Ant, what if the vicar thinks he still has a claim on the place? Perhaps he was looking for evidence when Tina saw him."

Ant leant on the open door of the Morgan, his interest engaged by Lyn's developing theory. "And don't forget that property developer. I think his name is Grindle. He certainly had a motive for wanting Ethan out of the way."

"Why?" replied Lyn.

He could see she was none too pleased as Ant seemed to cut across her theory about the vicar.

"Does the term 'ransom strip' mean anything to you, Lyn?"

From her facial expression, he guessed it didn't.

"It's when someone owns a piece of land that a developer needs before they can finalise a construction deal. In this case, the land Glebe Cottage stands on is the only access point onto the land Grindle presumably owns. If he doesn't secure Glebe Cottage, he can't develop the land. So you see, whoever *does* own the cottage can hold Grindle for ransom, so to speak."

Ant watched as a smile returned to Lyn's face.

Now the penny's dropped.

"You're saying that either the vicar or Grindle may have murdered Ethan? You know, so they could get their mitts on Glebe Cottage and demolish it? Perhaps they were in it together?"

Ant shook his head.

"No, I don't think the vicar murdered Ethan. It just doesn't fit."

He hesitated for a few seconds before continuing. "Then again, if he *did* find proof the church still owns the cottage and the land it stands on, then happy days, except—"

Lyn broke in.

"The vicar may be Grindle's next..."

9

SAINTS AND SINNERS

The frosted surface of Norwich Road glistened like a carpet of diamonds in the low morning sun as Ant drove to the village.

At least the Morgan's behaving, he thought as its engine purred beneath the bonnet.

Ant revelled in the village's laid-back Saturday routine. One minute he'd be slowing down to give a horse rider safe passage, the next, giving way to the postie on her rounds.

Love this place.

Two minutes later, he pulled into the forecourt of Fitch's Motor Repairs.

"Looks like you're busy," said Ant as he glanced around the cluttered space. A hotchpotch of vehicles filled the uneven, compacted earth and gravel yard.

"Always am, Ant. I keep my prices down and give top-notch service. Works for me," replied Fitch, while wiping his hands with the proverbial oily rag. "How's she running?"

Ant looked forlornly at the Morgan.

"Behaving for now but a sore point, and sort of why I'm here."

Ant watched as Fitch gave the car a quick once-over with his practised eye then shrugged his shoulders.

"It's not my company you're after, then," teased Fitch. "What's the problem?"

Ant reached into the passenger's seat and pulled out a wet towel.

"Ah, so you've been using the car as a portable shower, have you?" said Fitch.

Ant didn't see the funny side, a reaction he knew made Fitch enjoy the moment even more.

"Something like that. The thing is, I'm in Lyn's bad books. We went out for a drive last night. You know, soft top down, starry night, that kind of stuff. Then out of nowhere, it rains cats and dogs. I put the soft top up. Job done, you would think. Unfortunately, Lyn got soaked as I drove her home."

Fitch inspected the seam of the canvas covering, running his index finger along the soggy material.

"I don't want to say, 'I told you so,' but I told you so!" Remember me saying it needed waterproofing?"

Ant held his hands up in capitulation.

"Yes, yes, all right. Fair cop, guv. So have you got a can of that waterproofing spray stuff so I can fix the stupid thing or not?"

Ant knew his tone was bordering on the desperate.

"I have, but you'll have to wait for the top to dry or you'll be wasting your time. Anyway, serves you right. You know as well as I do that roaring around pitch-black roads in an old car is hardly Lyn's idea of a night out. You should have treated her to a meal or whatever romantic types do these days."

Ant frowned.

"That's enough of that. There's no boyfriend, girlfriend

stuff going on with Lyn. What are you thinking, mate? I mean—"

Fitch interrupted.

"What did that Shakespeare bloke say? 'He doth protest too much, methinks.'"

Ant cocked his head back and sniffed the air.

"To be strictly accurate, Fitch, I think you'll find Shakespeare talked about 'the lady,' not a 'he.' Anyway, moving on," said Ant without the trace of a smile. "What are you working on currently?"

Ant followed Fitch across the yard.

"There's a jammed tail lift on this van. It belongs to old Wilcox, and it's in a right old mess." Ant could just make out the faded name sign on the side of the box van:

Wilcox Removals and Storage.

Just then the sound of a car door banging caught both men's attention. A well-dressed man was leaning over his Morgan just outside the entrance to the garage.

"Do you know him, Fitch?"

The mechanic strained to see around his friend and glimpse the suited stranger.

"That's the bloke I was telling you about. His name is Stephen Grindle."

"Ah, yes. And that's his new Morgan Sports he's driving. Beautiful beast, isn't it? Must have cost a pretty penny. So he is our mysterious property developer, then."

Ant turned back to Fitch.

"It most certainly is; there must be a shed load of money in property to afford a car like that."

You're not wrong there, mate.

"Spot on, Fitch. Listen, I'll be back in a minute. I want a word with our friend. Let's see what he knows about Ethan's place."

Ant moved towards the yard entrance without waiting for a response from Fitch.

"Yours, is it? She's a beauty, no doubting that," said Grindle, pointing to Ant's car.

Ant looked back at his vintage Morgan.

"Yes, she is, and judging by what you're driving, I assume you're a fan too?"

Ant studied the stranger closely trying to get his measure. He knew the man was, in return, sizing him up.

"I've loved Morgan cars since I was a kid. Promised myself that if ever I made it, I'd buy one."

Ant watched Grindle stroke the front wing of his car as he spoke. It was if he were petting his favourite cat.

"Whatever you've made it in, it didn't take you long."

Can't be more than thirty, thought Ant as he silently admired the man's car.

"They're still handmade, you know."

Am I really that transparent?

"Have you done the factory tour?" he added. "Fascinating stuff. The café isn't half-bad either. I can recommend the cappuccino and lemon drizzle cake."

Grindle offered a thin smile. Ant could tell the stranger liked to be in control. He had come across such personalities many times. Bold front, brittle underneath.

Time for some fun, I think.

"No, I haven't. I've been meaning to go for years, but work and stuff always seems to get in the way."

He observed that Grindle's smile had slipped.

"Work? What does that mean to you?"

Ant noted the none too subtle change in Grindle's demeanour.

This is good.

"What do you think I do for a living, then?"

Ant's voice had an edge intended to tease.

"I doubt telling your servants what to do up at Stanton Hall takes much out of your day."

He's done his homework, but why so bitter? thought Ant.

He examined his opponent's expression. Grindle's cheeks twitched, indicating pent-up aggression.

He knows he's not reacting well. One more push, I think.

"Ah, I see. Another class warrior. As you say, instructing the servants on their daily duties does not take long."

Ant had adopted the same pantomime character he used on Detective Inspector Riley.

"The thing is, it leaves much more time for my other job. I don't do it for the money, you understand."

He watched as Grindle flushed. His nostrils began to flare.

"Other job?"

So he has trouble keeping his emotional intelligence in check under stress, does he?

"Oh, I dabble in land and related stuff. Now, what did you say you do?"

Ant's tone displayed a deliberate air of disinterest.

"Well, you've got enough of that. Land, I mean."

Sensing his opponent thought there might be a deal for the taking, Ant went in for the kill.

Got you.

"Oh no. You misunderstand, Mr Grindle, eh, Stephen, isn't it?"

Grindle nodded. Ant could tell the man was confused as to how he knew his first name.

"You see, I don't buy or sell land. The estate has been in the family for centuries, and well, we don't need the money, if you know what I mean?"

If only you knew the truth.

"When I say dabble, what I mean is that I specialise in planning anomalies. Fascinating topic, you know. I can't tell you how many shifty characters I come across who try to shaft some poor person out of their little house or whatever. Believe it or not, there are some people who will just stop at nothing to get their own way. Can you believe that, Stephen?"

Ant's domination of Grindle was complete.

"And what of you, Stephen? What did you succeed in so young to deliver this sort of wealth?"

Ant waved a hand in the general direction of Grindle's spotless Morgan.

"Property development. But—"

Ant purposely cut across Grindle.

"Oh dear, old chap. I do apologise."

He knew he was in danger of overacting but couldn't resist the temptation.

"Please forgive me speaking in such general terms. I didn't mean for a second to tar you with the same brush as the nastier elements of your profession. You do understand, don't you?"

Ant placed a hand on one of Grindle's elbows by way of reassurance. In fact, his intention was to reinforce his dominance.

He noted that Grindle tried to recoil from the physical contact.

A brittle personality indeed.

Within seconds, Grindle had regained his composure. Ant observed the first signs of the man's arrogance reasserting itself even if his eyes told a different story.

"No offence taken. After all, you weren't to know what I do for a living. Oh, and for the record, I conduct my business by the book."

Ant smiled to himself at Grindle's overemphasis on the overt reference to lawful trading.

"I'm sure you do," replied Ant as he extended his right hand.

Grindle reciprocated.

Handshake completed, the men parted company.

Ant watched as Grindle slid into his Morgan and marvelled at the low, masculine rumble of the exhaust as he disappeared into the distance.

"What was all that guff about you specialising in, what did you call it, 'planning anomalies'? And what about those bloody servants? You do talk a load of—"

Ant cut Fitch off, holding an open-palmed hand up to reinforce matters.

"As I've told you before, Fitch, look someone straight in the eye; talk with enough confidence, and they'll believe whatever you tell them. As for the servants, well, you're my mechanic, aren't you?"

Fitch made as if to doff an imaginary cap before retrieving the sodden towel from the forecourt floor.

"I believe this belongs to you, sir?"

Ant ducked as Fitch let fly.

Too late.

"Round two, I think, Fitch."

A split second later, Ant was pursuing his quarry at full pelt around the yard with the dripping towel flying between the two friends at regular intervals.

The chase ended when Ant's mobile rang.

"Do I have to?"

Ant watched Fitch stop in his tracks and noted he had the look of someone expecting to be tricked. The man had his arm out in a defensive position as if expecting his opponent to launch another attack with the filthy fabric.

"I will, yes: half past seven."

Ant pressed a key on the mobile to terminate the call.

"Bad news?"

"You could say that. Lyn's making me go to the quiz tonight at the village hall."

Fitch roared with laughter, made all the more enjoyable by a hardened military officer receiving orders from a head teacher.

"I don't know what you're laughing at. She said you have to come too."

10

QUIZ NIGHT

A nt walked at a brisk pace as he crossed High Street and held his collar up against the chilly evening wind. He turned the corner into Long Lane and walked down the narrow stone path that traced its way past an assortment of thatched cottages.

Two hundred yards ahead stood the village hall. Ant could see an array of multicoloured lights providing a welcome distraction from the leaden sky.

As he neared his destination, he caught sight of a strangely familiar figure.

Samantha. I wonder if she's feeling better now.

"Hi, good to see you again. How are you doing?"

Ant chose his tone carefully after seeing her so upset in the church.

He quickly realised that in the semi-darkness, Samantha hadn't seen him. Instead, the girl had her head down as she locked the wire-framed gates of Wilcox Removals and Storage.

"Oh, okay, thank you."

Samantha spoke hesitantly as she half looked at Ant

while turning the key in a heavy padlock. "It's kind of you to ask."

"Are you coming to the quiz?"

Ant checked himself realising how insensitive his question might appear.

He sensed Samantha was looking through rather than at him.

"Sorry, no. I need to get home. Dad will be waiting and..."

Ant's embarrassment grew. He wanted no repeat of the church situation.

"Of course. Of course. Do forgive me."

She smiled.

"Please. There's nothing to apologise for. Are *you* going to the quiz?"

Brave girl, thought Ant.

He admired her composure after her recent loss of her friend, Ethan.

"Yes, I am, although I hate quizzes. I always get the answers wrong. Let's walk together until I get to the hall, yes?"

Samantha didn't answer. Ant noticed the beginnings of a smile as she joined him.

The two walked in silence for a few seconds, neither looking at the other. Ant wasn't quite sure what to say.

It's either the weather or hobbies.

He opted for the latter.

"I don't suppose there's much for a young girl to do around the village, is there?"

It was the best he could come up with.

Samantha shook her head. It was what he'd expected since he'd felt the same at her age.

"No. Although there's the Sea Cadets I go to sometimes. They do some interesting stuff."

Ant worked hard to show interest. Anything to get her talking. He was pleased that her mood seemed to lighten as she explained the complexities of a sailing ship's rigging.

All too soon they reached the village hall.

"Well, I'd better get in, or my teammates will be after my scalp."

"And my dad will be expecting his tea," replied Samantha.

For the first time in their few minutes together, she gave him eye contact.

Ant took a step back, smiled, and gestured for the young woman to pass. Seconds later, he crossed the small car park of the village hall to see Lyn standing at the door making an exaggerated arm movement to look at her watch.

"Thought you'd got lost."

"Someone needed a bit of company." He didn't elaborate, and Lyn didn't enquire further, although he knew she'd seen him talking to Samantha.

"You're here, then."

Ant could just about hear the familiar voice above the general hubbub of the small space, having politely pushed himself through a throng of villagers. Turning to face Fitch, he saw Tina was with him. Ant acknowledged both with a friendly smile.

"Seems so."

Ant patted himself down as if checking all was present and correct.

"So this is our team, is it? Heaven help us. A retired soldier, a useless car mechanic, and a bossy head teacher. That just leaves you, Tina. At least you can spell and are used to organising a rabble."

Ant wore a look of mock resignation on his face.

"Speak for yourself," replied Lyn as she also strained to make herself heard above the noise.

Ant strained to look around the small hall. He knew the drill and shared everyone's irritation at being corralled at one end, since they were only allowed to take their allotted table on command of the quizmaster.

He could just about make out Jack Valentine, host for the evening, as he struggled to make his way onto the tiny stage. Ant, like everyone else, sometimes bridled at the man's officious manner but readily acknowledged that without him events such as tonight wouldn't happen.

"Testing, testing, one, two, three," said Jack. He then blew into the microphone for good measure, giving a passable impression he was suffering a bilious attack.

"Why does everyone who picks up a mic go through the same stupid routine?" protested Ant.

"Think it's as much about nerves as anything else," replied Tina.

"Do you remember that comic who built his whole act on pretending the microphone kept cutting out?" said Fitch.

Ant looked as puzzled at the other two.

"Is that one of tonight's questions?" joked Ant.

"Got you," replied Fitch. "It was Norman Collier. He was a great comic, wasn't he?"

Before Ant could reply, the sound of Jack's voice boomed around the wooden building.

"Ladies and Gentlemen, if there are any, that is. Please find your tables. The quiz is about to start."

Makes the same joke every time, thought Ant.

The hall erupted into a frenzy of movement as people scurried first one way then the other to locate their team's base.

As Ant neared their table, he felt a hand on his shoulder. Turning, he was surprised to be met by a smiling, young woman. For a split second he was unsure of who she was.

"Sally. Great to see you. Are you feeling better after your shock? And the baby?"

Ah, now I know who you are.

"It's been a hard few days for you, hasn't it? said Ant without letting slip he'd been momentarily confused, pleased that she hadn't seemed to have noticed.

"I'm fine and thanks, both of you. I know you're working like stink to find out what happened to poor Ethan. Oh, and yes, the baby, Dr Thorndike says he... or she... is absolutely fine. Thanks for asking."

Ant glanced at the two women who were exchanging contented smiles.

Well, that's all right, then.

A semblance of order soon returned as the noise level reduced to a low buzz as heads bent towards the centre of team tables to finalise tactics.

Responsibilities allocated and pencil checks completed, the assembly readied itself for battle.

Jack's tone changed as he asked the first question. He spoke in a low, serious voice, as if he were about to deliver a four-minute warning of impending doom.

"Your first question. Which British general met his end at Khartoum?"

Ant took careful note of a player at the next table.

"I know this. It's Gordon Ramsey," said the excited man.

He noticed Lyn giving him the eye.

"You're not serious, are you? For heaven's sake, Ant, you're a military man. You should know this."

Above the hubbub, he attempted to defend himself.

"Don't be daft. She's talking rubbish. It's Alf, not Gordon Ramsey."

Ant looked mystified as he watched his teammates almost fall off their chairs laughing. He gave Fitch a particularly hard stare.

"What?"

"Ant, you're nearly right... and very wrong. The former is a chef, but the latter was England's football manager at the 1966 World Cup."

Ant wore a perplexed look as he plundered his brain for the military history that had been drummed into him at Sandhurst.

"Give up?" asked Fitch.

He continued before Ant had time to react.

"The answer is Charles Gordon. You know, 'Gordon of Khartoum.'"

Ant thumped the centre of his forehead with an open palm. He could see Fitch had a look of expectancy.

"What do you want, Fitch, a *Kinder Surprise*?"

"You can keep your chocolate egg, Ant. It means the first round of drinks are on you."

"THANK HEAVENS THAT'S OVER. My head hurts."

Ant massaged his temple for emphasis as the first part of the evening came to a welcomed end. He shivered in the chilled air as he and his three companions gathered just outside the rear door of the hall. They had a job to dodge the fog of tar and nicotine from a huddled group of middle-aged locals standing opposite.

I hate second-hand smoke.

Ant frowned at the smokers and gave an exaggerated

cough. No words were exchanged, but his acting skills were enough for the offenders to move away from the door and shuffle farther onto the car park like a waddle of penguins bracing themselves against a blizzard.

"Reminded me of those horrible school spelling tests," said Fitch.

Ant nodded, raised an arm above his head then brought it down as if striking something.

"You're not wrong there. Remember our English teacher, Stinger Cumberland, and that stiff leather strap he hid up his jacket sleeve?"

Ant watched Fitch shudder, Lyn laugh, and Tina frown.

"Called it his 'stinger,' didn't he?"

Ant pointed to the back of his left hand.

"Too right he did. You got a whack across here for each spelling you got wrong. Flaming hurt, that strap did."

"And never on the right hand so you could keep writing. Can't imagine that happening now."

"It does not, Fitch. Anyway, it didn't work since both of you are still atrocious at spelling. Am I correct?"

Ant looked at Fitch as they both broke out into laughter.

"No, and I still hate the smell of leather."

"My point exactly, Ant. Not the leather bit, of course," said Lyn, trying to make a serious point. "Corporal punishment, I mean. Just useless and wrong."

Ant looked at his other two companions as a combined smirk broke out.

"Now then, Head Teacher. You're quite right. We're only winding you up, even if I do still bear the scars."

He glanced at the back of his left hand and pulled a faux sad face.

"Hmm," huffed Lyn. Ant watched as the expression on her face changed from mate to headmistress. The more severe her look became, the funnier he and the others found it.

"Ladies and Gentlemen, if there are any," said the quizmaster.

His stale joke met with a universal groan. "Part two will begin in three minutes. That's three minutes. I thank you."

"Why does he always have to be so precise. It drives me nuts."

"His father was an accountant, Ant. I think that might have something to do with it," said Fitch.

The others gave Fitch a bemused look.

"What?"

"Fitch, his dad was a bookie who went bankrupt, which in my mind has to be a first."

Ant winked at Lyn and Tina, who were already ahead of him. He then placed a reassuring arm around Fitch and ruffled his friend's hair with his free hand.

"Come on, we'd better go in for the second half. Look, the throng is almost upon us."

Ant pointed to the smokers who were taking a synchronised final drag on their cigs, and a crush of villagers headed for the open entrance.

Ant raced ahead with Fitch. He had no intention of taking a pummelling from Phyllis, Betty, and the other formidable elder stateswomen of the village. He was wise enough to know they were not to be messed with.

"Did you manage to fix that van you were working on earlier, Fitch?"

His friend opened both arms as if describing the size of a fish he'd caught.

"Yes, but you wouldn't believe the damage a piece of old hemp that size could do."

Ant nodded, though he didn't quite understand Fitch's

point. He struggled to hear his friend over the frenzy of excited villagers as they took their seats and waited for the quizmaster to do his thing.

STEPHEN GRINDLE PARKED his Morgan outside Glebe Cottage. In the darkness he peered at the lonely building. Shadows danced across the flint wall like backlit glove puppets acting out some crazy slapstick routine.

He waited as his car's hands-free telephone system played the call tone.

Grindle tapped the steering wheel with both hands and played an imaginary drum riff as his frustration grew.

At last the call connected. He didn't wait for the other person to finish speaking.

"I'm sat here doing nothing, that's what. Where are you?"

His tone was angry, his patience exhausted. He'd had enough.

"We need to meet and sort this deal out once and for all. I've too much money sunk into it to let it go now. Do you understand?"

11

SUNDAY LUNCH

"I'm sorry the chocolate cake is a day late," said Lyn as she handed Ant her coat.

Walking across the oak-boarded floor, her steps fell silent as she crossed onto the lush pile of a hearth rug. She stood behind two occupied dining chairs in their prime position in front of the warming, open fire.

Lyn placed a hand on each chair back and leant forward before planting a warm kiss on the Earl of Stanton's cheek. She turned and landed an affectionate peck on Ant's mother's cheek.

"Not to worry, you do spoil us with your wonderful baking, my dear," replied the earl, his voice bright as a button. "Nice you're able to join us for Sunday lunch, and we now have our sweet!"

Lyn watched the earl's face light up with delight.

"Hope you don't mind us eating in here instead of the dining room. As you know, this used to be the drawing room in the old days. It's much cosier than the other room."

"I think it's a great idea. There's nothing better than a

roaring fire that you can feel on your cheeks on a day like this," replied Lyn.

She'd listened to the same story about the origin of the room by the old lady many times. It didn't bother Lyn in the slightest.

"I'll serve."

Not waiting for a response, Lyn opened the hostess trolley and accepted Ant's offer to help dish up the piping-hot meal.

"Such a good idea, those warming cabinet thingies, aren't they?" said Ant's father. "It was the cook's idea and means she can prepare food for us without having to hang around while we old duffers shuffle our bones."

A PITILESS WIND blew off the North Sea, courtesy of the Russian Steppes. Keen to escape its ravages, Ant and Lyn took full advantage of the shelter offered by the walled garden.

As they walked their lunch off, both were in a reflective mood.

"Your mum sounded tired, Ant. Gerald looked a bit distracted too. Is everything all right?"

Ant pulled the few remaining leaves off a rose bush overhanging the gravel path.

"You know Mum and Dad. The doctor tells them to take it easy, and what do they do? Dig over a new flower border. In their mid-eighties and thrashing about with spades. I ask you."

Lyn's gaze followed Ant's finger as he pointed to a tiny patch of newly cultivated earth.

Lyn picked up on Ant's intonation in a heartbeat.

"So that's what Dr Thorndike's visit was all about."

She watched as Ant stopped his impromptu hand pruning and pivoted his head towards her.

"I didn't say he'd called when I mentioned him to you the other day."

She knew he was being defensive.

Lyn fixed Ant with a look he was unable to ignore.

"You didn't need to. I know you better than you know yourself sometimes."

Lyn's smile, and the sincerity in her voice disarmed Ant. It always did.

They continued their stroll as each reminisced about childhood certainties and always having parents around.

Except as grown-ups, they knew these things were an illusion.

"But they're as happy as Larry, you know, Lyn. Apart from Dad's war service, they've never spent a night apart. Can you believe that? I dread to think what will happen when one of them goes."

Lyn could see how Ant struggled with the thought and watched as he fell silent for a few seconds.

"And your parents, Lyn?"

Lyn shrugged her shoulders. "Do you know, they still can't spend more than two minutes in each other's company without arguing. Why one or the other doesn't move out of the village is beyond me."

"Parents. We moan about them when they're here. Can't bear to think about losing them, Lyn."

Lyn turned towards Ant, exchanging a look that needed no further explanation.

"Right, enough of this depressing stuff. Let's talk about murder," said Ant.

Lyn couldn't help but laugh at the irony.

"I love your idea about what's depressing and what isn't, Ant."

Lyn followed her host into a small summer house in the far corner of the walled garden.

"Heavens, thank the Lord it's warmer in here out of that easterly," said Lyn.

The pair strolled to one end of the rickety, wood-and-glass structure.

"I have a confession, Ant. I often come in here after I've dropped your mum and dad's chocolate cake off on a Saturday."

Ant cocked his head to one side and reached down to retrieve something from the floor.

"I know you do."

A quizzical look spread across her face.

"How?"

She looked on as Ant held up the item he'd retrieved from the herringbone-patterned brick floor.

"I only know one person who eats black-and-white, mint humbugs around here." He held up an empty sweet wrapper.

"Heaven knows how you manage to eat those things without pulling your teeth out."

Lyn worked hard on her guilty look as she snatched at the empty wrapper.

"I admit it, you've caught me red handed. As for preserving one's molars—secret is to warm them in your pocket first."

Lyn pointed to her cheek to emphasise the point.

"I didn't know you wore dentures?"

His smile gave away his intentional misinterpretation of Lyn's words.

"Clever clogs. You know what I mean."

She tossed the empty wrapper at Ant, who, failing to duck in time, felt the wrapper tickle as it bounced off his forehead and returned to the floor whence it came.

Lyn's smile broadened with the satisfaction of knowing her aim remained accurate.

"Speaking of clever clogs, have you spoken to your boyfriend yet, Lyn?"

Lyn bristled, which was the reaction she knew Ant had intended to elicit.

"You know full well I haven't seen him since Noah was a lad."

A scowl spread across Lyn's face.

Ant shrugged his shoulders, raised his chin an inch or two, and shook his head, closing his eyes as he did so.

"Whatever," he replied, hoping Lyn would bite.

Surmising as much, Lyn did not react and waited for Ant to open his eyes. He fell for her trap as she knew he would.

"You're back with us, then?"

Lyn busied herself inspecting her nail varnish for non-existent chips while savouring Ant's tactical failure.

"But as luck and good fortune would have it, yes, I did have a chat with him."

Lyn adopted a disinterested tone, making no attempt to offer further information.

Seconds, which seemed to feel like minutes, passed as Lyn and Ant stared each other out. She knew he would give in first.

"Fair enough. You win. Now let's have the rest of it."

Lyn laughed.

"You're hopeless. Never could stare me out, even at school, could you?"

Lyn was enjoying Ant's defeat.

"How many times must I tell you, I wasn't the one who told old *Slab Head* you let his tyres down."

Hands on hips, her gaze holding firm, she had no intention of letting him off the hook just yet.

"Who mentioned the tyres? Anyway, I met our old headmaster years later. He told me he knew it was Alfie Hemmings all the time. You know, the lad who used to suck his thumb in class."

Lyn detected Ant's intrigue at the new startling news.

"He said he put me in detention because I cleaned the blackboards better than anyone else. It seemed the headmaster needed them doing for the school governors' visit the next day."

"And you let me think it was my fault all these years. You—"

"Now then. No swearing, Lord Stanton. Remember your station in life. Anyway, it serves you right for thinking the worst of me."

As the two friends squared up to each other, Lyn still held the upper hand.

"Wait a minute," said Ant.

Lyn laughed and pointed at Ant as he adopted an exaggerated gait.

"Who do you think you are? Henry VIII?"

Lyn's hilarity didn't last long as Ant hit on a connection.

"Wait a minute. That boyfriend of yours in the planning department is called Alfie, isn't he?"

Lyn blushed as Ant let out a roar of laughter.

"No wonder he's sweet on you. He thinks you took the rap all those years ago to save him from detention. I seem to remember he was always hanging around you like a puppy with his thumb stuck in his gob."

Lyn failed to see the funny side of Ant's deduction.

"Do you want to know what the man told me or not?"

Her tone confirmed she was in no mood for Ant's theatrics. Nevertheless, she had to wait for what seemed like ages before Ant had settled enough to take in Lyn's offer.

"Right. Shall I start, then?"

Lyn unfolded her arms.

"Grindle Developments has submitted an outline-planning application to build twelve executive, five-bedroom homes and four starter properties on the land behind Ethan's cottage."

She knew this information would bring Ant to his senses.

"What's more, and as you expected, the application shows road access to the development right through the cottage."

"Aha. Told you so. But answer me this. Why would Grindle invest time and money on a planning application when he doesn't own Glebe Cottage?"

Lyn frowned then shrugged her shoulders.

"Perhaps he's done a deal with someone. But who?"

"There's one way to find out, Lyn. Here's what I think we should do."

12

THE GREASY SPOON

"And what are we looking for exactly?"

Fitch failed to hide his irritation at being press-ganged into trudging through Stanton Woods.

"Do you never stop moaning?" replied Ant. "Anyway, you were the one that offered to come if I bought you breakfast."

Ant craned his neck as he surveyed the leaf-covered car park that gave access to the woods. He'd been careful to park his Morgan in the far corner of the small clearing so that he didn't contaminate possible evidence.

"Mind where you're walking, for heaven's sake."

Ant's caution caused Fitch to freeze as if he were about to step on a landmine. Turning to face his friend, he stuck both hands in his pockets and shrugged his shoulders.

"Go on, then. Give us a clue. Permission to move, sir."

Ant raised an eyebrow, unimpressed with Fitch's supposed comedy impression of a squaddie.

"Get yourself over here, and tell me what you can see."

Both men now stood side by side looking down the narrow track. Beyond, lay the spot where Ethan had been found.

"See them?"

Ant crouched as he spoke, leaving Fitch to look down at him in bemusement.

Ant's gaze veered between the trackway and the strengthening sun. His interest lay in how its rays forced their way through a tangle of branches in the tree canopy and hit the ground.

"This isn't doing my knees any good."

"Don't be a softy, Fitch. Now kneel down next to me."

Ant prompted Fitch to close one eye then the other, and tell him what he could see.

"What, you mean those parallel lines?"

Ant was impressed. He'd done much better than Lyn when asked the same question.

"Well done, Fitch. Yes, two parallel depressions leading up the track."

He pointed a finger to trace their progression into the woods.

"They're just a set of wheel marks from one of your forestry buggies, Ant. Nothing special, I'd say."

He reached forward to disturb a compressed strip of leaves in front of him.

"No, no. You're not getting it, Fitch."

Ant pointed again towards the trackway.

"Wait here, and I'll show you."

Ant walked forward in a semicircular movement. As he did so, he picked up four twigs, each about twelve inches long.

"See it now?"

Ant had laid a twig across the depressions to show their depth.

"Caused by something much heavier than one of our estate vehicles."

Ant encouraged his friend to focus on the four twigs a few feet apart, two on each track.

"Good Lord. You're right. Something bigger than a quad bike made those, that's for sure."

Ant smiled.

"There you go. The next question is, why drive something that big down this track. There's no evidence of trees being cut down, so they haven't nicked any of the estate's timber. So what else might they have been doing?"

Ant stood next to Fitch in silence for a few seconds as they focused on the tracks.

"We can say for sure whatever it was that made the tracks was heavy. But what type of vehicle do you think it was, Fitch?"

Ant turned to look at his friend.

"Judging by the width between the tyre marks and their depth, I'd say a commercial vehicle."

Ant nodded.

"And a tall one at that."

Fitch looked at his friend then back at the tracks.

"What makes you say that?"

"They do."

Fitch's eyes followed Ant's index finger.

It pointed to a neat row of snapped branches six feet above them.

LYN WAS ABOUT to give up on Ant's instruction to find Stephen Grindle and head back to work until she drove past a lay-by opposite the entrance to Home Farm. She could see Lil's greasy spoon chuck wagon was having a busy time of it.

Lyn glimpsed Grindle's gleaming sports car.

So there you are.

Pulling over, she parked her Mini in a muddy passing point on the narrow lane and headed back towards the lay-by. As she neared, Lyn spotted Grindle. He had his back to the road and was drinking from a polystyrene cup while seemingly deep in conversation on his mobile.

Keen to remain hidden from her quarry, Lyn dodged the parked lorries and made her way to the chuck wagon.

"Not seen you for a while, Lyn," said Lil.

Lyn smiled at the petite woman who wore a pristine, white apron and blue vinyl gloves.

"It's not for the want of trying, Lil. Hard to get away from school these days. May I have a coffee?"

SHE WATCHED as Lil busied herself scraping the excess cooking oil and bacon fat from a hotplate.

"You can have a china mug. The lads get the polystyrene version. It saves on the washing up!"

Lil winked as she handed Lyn her drink.

"Nice to talk to another lady for a change," added Lil with a throaty laugh.

Lyn appreciated the china mug and Lil's words.

"Get away with you. You love every minute of it. From what I've heard, the drivers think the world of you, especially when you shout at them."

In some ways, Lyn envied Lil. Twenty years her own boss. Worked when she wanted and out in the open air.

Good on you, girl, thought Lyn. She knew Lil had fought hard for the success she now enjoyed.

"Not seen anything of your ex, then, Lil?"

Lil was busy wringing out a clean dishcloth as Lyn's words hit. She let out a throaty laugh and gave the cloth an extra squeeze as if it were some part of her ex-husband's anatomy.

"No, glad to say. The best day's work I ever did was chucking that fool out. And you know what the funniest thing is?"

Lyn cupped her mug of coffee and came closer to the counter to get out of the wind. She waited in anticipation of the caterer's next revelation.

"The ratbag he left me for has got him right under her thumb. Serves the bugger right, if you ask me. He didn't know which side his bread was buttered; that was his problem."

Lyn could see Lil meant every word and spoke without a hint of regret or jealousy.

As Lyn listened, she caught a movement out of the corner of her eye. Grindle had climbed back into his car.

Hell's bells.

"Talking of bread and butter. Can you do me a bacon-and-egg bap, Lil? I'll be back in a minute."

She made off towards Grindle, greeting him with a cheery "Hello."

"Lyn Blackthorn, isn't it?"

Lyn waited for him to clamber out of the open-topped Morgan. "Thank you for doing such a wonderful job. Educating young minds is so important, isn't it?"

Lyn failed to hide her surprise. He looked dapper, sounded genuine, and had a sparkle in his eye. She could see why some women might find him attractive.

"Well, er, thank you. Yes, I suppose, well, of course I know you're right. About education, I mean."

She could feel herself blushing.

Why is he making me feel like a teenager?

An awkward silence developed as Lyn thought of what to say next without raising his suspicions.

"Now then, a few ladies mentioned they'd seen you around the village. You know what it's like in a small place like Stanton Parva. Handsome young man, posh car and all that. Now what we all want to know is, are you here to see a secret lady friend, or is it just silly business?"

Lyn hoped she'd put Grindle off the trail since he seemed to lap up her compliments like a cat having got the cream.

Grindle smiled and looked her up and down from head to foot.

I hate people who do that, thought Lyn as she endured his inspection. She was unsure if he did it out of habit or by design to unnerve his opponent.

"Oh dear. What is a man to say?"

You're a smooth one.

She noted his failure to bite on her question so tried a different tack.

"My mother thinks you're going to build them a nice big supermarket on the old petrol station site. If you do, I guess it'll make you the most popular man around here amongst us girls. It's fifteen miles and twenty minutes each way at the moment."

Lyn watched as Grindle's look intensified, and his smile morphed into a look of concern.

My my, you are a slick operator.

"Well, Ms Blackthorn, you never know." Grindle touched the side of his nose with a finger as if sharing a state secret. Speaking of which, I need to be off. You know—things to do, people to see."

Without further words exchanged, Lyn extended her

right hand. Grindle reciprocated. Seconds later he was gone, leaving her to ponder what he was really up to.

"Your bap's ready."

Lyn turned in the direction of the voice to see Lil hanging out of the chuck wagon, bacon-and-egg feast in hand.

Ten minutes later, Lyn was back in the Mini driving back into the village.

That's interesting.

Lyn had caught sight of Reverend Morton talking to a man she didn't recognise, outside Glebe Cottage. As she neared, the stranger moved off towards the village centre.

What's the vicar up to?

She pulled alongside the clergyman and wound down the window.

"Good morning, Vicar."

Lyn liked the fact that her sudden arrival had taken him by surprise. She could tell from his delayed response that he was trying to gather his thoughts.

"Oh, Lyn. There you are. Sorry if I seem a little absent minded today. I'm in a world of my own, you know."

Lyn smiled as if to give the vicar permission to compose himself.

"I just wanted to catch up with you to discuss your next talk to the children. They do love your visits to the school so much."

She watched as the vicar frowned.

"Well, yes, we can, if you wish. It's usually your secretary that finalises these things with me. The only thing is I'm a bit pushed for time just now."

Reverend Morton glanced at his wristwatch and twiddled the winder between his finger and thumb. Lyn was aware his agitation was increasing as the seconds passed.

What are you up to, I wonder, Reverend?

"Oh, I see. No problem at all. I can tell you're busy. I'll get Tina to ring you, shall I?"

Reverend Morton didn't need a second invitation to make his escape.

"People to see, you know."

Lyn waved as the reverend hurried off, still looking at his watch.

That's the second time I've heard that expression this morning.

13

NIGHT WALKING

"When you rang to ask if I fancied a walk, you didn't say I'd need my wellies."

Ant looked on as Lyn gazed at her feet.

I'm guessing rubber boots are not her idea of high fashion.

He laughed as they made their way from the back garden of Lyn's cottage onto the school field that lay beyond.

"Well, what would you rather do on a wet Monday night, Lyn? Anyway, I heard tell you were one of those women with a fetish for rubber?"

Ant put a sprint on, hoping to avoid retribution.

Clambering over the low drystone wall, Ant fell forward.

She's pushed me!

"The only fetish I've got is for the plaster you'll need when I've finished with you. Cheeky devil."

Ant let out a muffled scream as he hit the sodden ground with a dull thud.

"Are you okay?" whispered Lyn. "Ant, are you all right? For goodness' sake, say something."

Ant let out a low moaning noise. Face contorted with pain, he held a hand to his chest.

Ant fell silent as Lyn knelt over him until her face almost touched his.

"Boo."

Ant's sudden outburst caused Lyn to fall backwards and let out a strangled scream. He roared with laughter as she landed in a muddy depression with her wellington boot soles pointing to the heavens.

"That's what you get for occasioning actual bodily harm on your best mate, young lady."

His amusement continued as he scrambled to his feet, pulling Lyn up with him.

"One of these days, Anthony, one of these days."

He watched as Lyn brushed herself down and wagged a finger at him.

"Anyway, enough of this larking about. We've work to do, Lyn."

Ant caught Lyn's best head-teacher glare, shrugged his shoulders, and responded with his little-boy-lost look.

"You started it."

He gave a throaty laugh.

"Do you realise you sound just like one of your seven-year-olds?"

He watched the first signs of a smile spreading across Lyn's face.

"Whatever."

Both laughed and bumped shoulders.

Within a minute, the back of Glebe Cottage began to reveal itself as the pair trudged across the drenched ground. Set against a dark, sullen sky, Ant focused on the stark silhouette of the forlorn-looking cottage as if it were waiting to be reclaimed by the master who would never return.

"So tell me again, Ant. Just why are we getting soaked to the skin on this freezing-cold evening?"

Ant looked puzzled as his friend bent down, before spotting her attempt to loosen a small stone trapped between the ball of her foot and wellie sole.

"You have a memory like a sieve at times, Lyn. So my pathologist mate confirmed a second rope burn around Ethan's neck. If my hunch is correct, he was dead before he got anywhere near that tree."

He could see the horror of his suggestion beginning to dawn on his friend.

I wish I could take this away from her.

"You're saying Ethan died somewhere other than in the woods?"

Ant stopped and turned to Lyn and pointed to the flint-faced rear wall of Ethan's place.

"Could have happened anywhere, his cottage, for example."

The shudder Lyn gave meant Ant could see she now understood what their night caper was about.

"I know. Makes you think, doesn't it?"

Ten feet farther on, and they had reached the back gate of the cottage. Ant lifted the latch and stood to one side while Lyn passed through into Ethan's garden.

They stood rooted to the spot for a few seconds and watched shadows dance across the back wall of the humble chocolate-box building, as angry clouds first hid then revealed the moon in the gathering wind. The effect was soporific.

Could somewhere as beautiful as this really have been used to take a life? thought Ant.

"So if I'm right, there may just be something in there to tell us what happened that night."

Once they had reached the rear door to the property, Ant pulled four plastic bags from his coat.

"Here, put these on."

Ant handed Lyn two pedal-bin liners.

Lyn watched as he placed each of his booted feet into a bag.

"What on earth—"

"We don't want to tread mud all through Ethan's place, now, do we? Anyway, better no one knows we've been here."

Taking advantage of Ant's firm frame, Lyn rested a hand on his shoulder to steady herself as she pulled the plastic bags over her footwear.

Ant considered had a stranger crossed their path at that moment, they may have supposed the pair were involved in some ancient village ritual. He struggled to support both himself and Lyn as they swayed from side to side, perching on first one leg then the other and at the same time trying to tuck the plastic coverings into the tops of their wellies.

As Ant expected, once their eyes met, gallows humour took over as they collapsed in a heap against the sturdy rear door.

Got to get a grip, or we've had it.

"Come on, Lyn. No time for larking about. Someone might see us, and then we'll have some explaining to do."

His gentle reproach worked, eventually. He watched as Lyn struggled to regain her composure.

Rummaging around in his jacket pocket, he retrieved a set of keys then two short sticks made of transparent plastic.

Lyn's bemused look almost made him start giggling again.

"Here, take this," he whispered.

Ant handed Lyn one of the sticks.

"Twist it."

"What do you mean?"

"Lyn, just do it, or we'll be here all night."

A soft, thin beam of light bathed a small area of the door as Lyn complied with his instruction.

"Won't see it from outside once we're in. Clever bit of kit, eh?"

He watched as Lyn interrogated the stick light. She hadn't seen anything quite like it.

"Is this one of your spy gadgets?"

She waved the light around and giggled.

Ant fixed her with a stern look, his smile gone.

"If I tell you, I'll have to kill you."

Ant couldn't keep up the pretence for more than a couple of seconds.

"Is that so, Mr Bond?" quipped Lyn. "And those? I suppose they're some sort of sonic device for opening locks?"

Ant jangled the metal objects.

"Nope, just my house keys."

Ant noticed Lyn sigh as he put the keys back in his pocket and produced a small, stiff card.

A few seconds later, a crisp *click* pierced the silence, and Ant gently pushed the door open just enough to allow access. He smiled triumphantly.

"Impressive, eh? After you."

Passing through the kitchen and into the hallway, the pair hesitated before entering the lounge. It was as if it had been a jolly caper until now. But beyond the door, Ant expected to see the everyday things Ethan would have used and enjoyed.

He opened the oak-stained pine door. It took a few seconds for his eyes to adjust to the dark shapes in the room. He checked Lyn, who nodded to confirm all was well.

"Someone's beaten us to it."

Ant surveyed a scene of devastation. All around lay

papers that had been flung from the fitments that lined the room. Not a square foot of carpet remained free of detritus.

"What do you think they were looking for, Ant?"

He scanned the room a second time by shining his light across the chaotic scene.

"That rather depends on if whoever did this was here before or after Ethan died."

He saw Lyn shaking her head.

"It's a right mess, isn't it, Lyn?"

Ant doubted she'd taken in his words. She looked utterly lost in the moment.

"Or during the..."

Her voice tailed off.

"The murder. No, Lyn. If it helps, I don't think it happened here. This is a burglary, or it's staged to look like one. But there's no sign of a struggle—or anything else."

Ant fell silent. He knew Lyn would understand what he meant. Then a beam of light permeated the thin curtains of the front bay window.

Ant gently took hold of Lyn's arm as much to indicate she should stay still as for reassurance.

"Someone's coming," whispered Ant. "Move over to the hall door, but don't go through until I tell you."

Lyn stood rooted to the position Ant had told her to take up.

He moved towards the window. Shielding himself to the side, he slowly pulled a small section of the curtain back.

"Hell's bells. It's Riley. What the dickens is he doing here?"

It wasn't meant as a question for Lyn. If anything, he was reflecting how wise it had been, in the first place, to gain entrance to what he could plainly see was a crime scene.

Ant watched the detective inspector leave his police car and begin to walk up the front path of the cottage.

"Get ready to move... No, wait."

Just as he was about to join Lyn and escape the scene, Ant watched as something flashed in Riley's hand. The detective stopped, looked at the light, then lifted his hand to his right ear.

"He's taking a call. This is our chance to slip away. There's nothing more for us in here, Lyn."

Ant gestured for Lyn to ready herself for the short dash back through the kitchen and out into the back garden of the cottage.

He watched as Lyn ran.

Thank goodness for that. The fool's back in his car. Must have been called away to another job.

Ant let out a nervous laugh before realising Lyn re-entered the kitchen and was urging him on with an outstretched arm.

"Another lucky escape, Houdini. One of these days your luck will run out, then let's see whether being a lord makes any difference."

Ant laughed again, gave an exaggerated bow, and took Lyn's outstretched hand as she turned towards the back door.

Then came a noise that made them both freeze solid. Ant pointed his light stick at the floor. One of them had kicked something against the plinth of the kitchen units.

He crouched down.

"It's a pen. Always come in handy, do pens."

Ant stuffed it into his jacket pocket before following Lyn out of the building, taking great care to lock the back door and check that it was in the same condition in which they'd found it.

Satisfied all was well, he turned to Lyn who was pointing at her feet.

"Can we take these stupid plastic bags off now?"

He raised his index finger and wagged it at Lyn.

"Better to wear a plastic bag than spend a night in the police cells, don't you think?"

His look said it all.

"Whatever," Lyn replied.

He could see she was determined not to bite.

As the pair trudged back across the field, Ant noticed movement from a factory separated from the field by a high wire fence.

"Someone's working late."

His attention was drawn to a slim figure clambering out of a box van.

"Poor devil, I bet they're getting peanuts to work overtime," said Lyn.

Ant huffed.

"If it's their own business, I suspect they aren't getting paid at all."

14

BAD BUSINESS

"Not a job for the faint hearted, is it?"

Fitch offered a friendly smile as Brian Wilcox made polite conversation while they stood with their backs to a piercing east wind on the garage forecourt.

"You're not wrong there. That blessed wind goes straight through me."

Fitch gave an involuntary shiver while wiping a small gathering of phlegm from the end of his reddened nose.

"You'd think we'd get used to this blasted weather, being so close to sea. Well, my bones say different, Brian."

He gave a sharp tug on his woollen bob cap to provide a little comfort for his stinging ears then slammed the bonnet of a car that had seen better days.

"Come on, let's get out of this weather," said Fitch as he led the way into his office.

"Sorry about the mess, mate. Sit where you can." Fitch glanced around the tiny space, every surface piled high with car parts and oil-stained paperwork.

"I guess your place is just as bad. Us mechanical types are all the same, aren't we?"

Brian's smile provided Fitch with the response he'd expected.

"Don't include me in that. Everything in its place and a place for everything. That's what I say."

Fitch turned to see a familiar figure racing through the rickety doorway.

"Good day, Mr Perfect. Born in a barn, were you? Now shut that flaming door, so I can keep the heat in."

He gave a wry smile as his friend shook his head and pointed to a broken pane of glass in the door.

"All right, smarty pants. There's a difference between controlled ventilation and a hurricane, you know. Now what brings you out from the lap of luxury on a cold Tuesday morning?"

"If you think Stanton Hall in an easterly is a great place to be, you're welcome to it. Fancy a swap?"

Fitch knew Ant had a point.

"You must be mad. Your place is a money pit. At least all I need to do is spend ten quid on a bit of glass and it's job done." He matched Ant's smile before realising he'd almost forgotten Brian was there.

"Apologies for my friend's interruption. You know what upper-class types are like."

Fitch smiled at Brian knowing it was all the man could do to acknowledge the lighthearted exchange with a modest nod.

"Oh, you know. Just wanted to see what the real world was up to," said Ant.

Fitch gestured for Ant to sit down and smiled as his friend breezed across the cluttered space, lifted a broken steering wheel from a rickety metal chair, and plonked himself down.

"Don't believe a word he says, Brian. Although you can

eat your dinner off the floor of his workshop. That's down to his father. Anyway, you should have seen him at school. He was the most disorganised kid going."

Again, Fitch's intention was to include Brian in the banter.

Poor Brian.

Fitch soldiered on, leading an animated discussion on three subjects: the weather, how useless politicians were, and the price of diesel.

Oops, made a booby there.

"Well, I'll leave you both to it. Thanks for fixing the van."

Fitch watched as Brian looked at his invoice, folded the piece of paper into four, and tucked it into an inside pocket of his faded waxed jacket.

"Keep safe, Brian. Chin up, mate."

The mechanic couldn't help but watch Brian trudge forlornly across the yard, pulling his collar up against the biting wind before disappearing into the distance. He sighed as he turned, threw the dregs of two chipped coffee mugs onto a pile of used kitchen towels then refilled them from a grimy percolator.

"He's a proud man and as honest as the day, but he's in big trouble," said Fitch as he handed Ant the cleaner of the two mugs. He looked on as his visitor skimmed a film of something or other from its surface and commented.

"I thought he looked a bit down. Do you think he'll be okay?"

Fitch drank from his mug without skimming its surface.

"Transport's a hard game at the best of times, Ant. Did you see his face when we mentioned diesel going up in price again? I could have kicked myself."

Fitch sucked air through the gap in his front teeth to emphasise the point.

"As your dad has said to me more times over the years than I care to remember—if you run out of money in business, you're finished. Doesn't matter how full your order book is. If you've no cash to service the work, it's goodnight Vienna."

"Are you saying he's broke?"

Fitch glanced at his old friend. There were times when he thought it impossible for Ant to understand how the "other half" lived.

"That's exactly what I'm saying, Ant. When you're a one-man band, it isn't just the business that cops it. I bet he's sold his soul to the bank like most of us have to. If his removal business *does* go bust, those bloodsuckers will be on him like a pack of hounds. He'll lose everything, including his home, I bet."

Fitch spoke with an uncharacteristic bitterness. But then he'd seen what bankruptcy had done to his father and its long-lasting effects on the rest of the family.

"Are you sure you're right?"

Fitch shrugged his shoulders.

"Look, I may be jumping at shadows, but I see the signs. I hear he owes money to suppliers all over the place—including me. It's only his good name that's kept Brian going for so long. The thing is, Ant, I don't know whether we're doing him any favours."

"So you won't get paid for fixing his van?"

Fitch shook his head, more in sadness than anything else.

"At least his daughter looks after him. She dotes on the man. Mind you, after losing her mum so early, you can understand why she sticks to him like glue. You, more than most, know what losing a close family member is like."

Not quite thinking through what he'd said, Fitch gave

Ant an anxious glance, only to see his friend nodding in agreement and downing the last of his coffee, seemingly unperturbed by the comparison.

"Enough of this gloom," said Ant. "What's your next job?"

Distracted by the moment, Fitch failed to answer.

"Hello, anyone home?"

Fitch turned.

"I did hear you, you know. "The vicar's Volvo, if you must know. In a hell of a state. No pun intended, of course."

Fitch smiled even though he knew better than to laugh at his own jokes.

Quite clever that, if I say so myself.

Ant's moan, as if he'd just read a corny joke from a Christmas cracker, caused Fitch to enjoy the interlude even more.

"What's he been up to, then?"

Fitch pointed as he looked out of the office window, which was hardly fulfilling its purpose in keeping the rain out. Covered with a thick layer of greasy grime as it was, he could just about make out the vicar's Volvo.

"He's done his rear suspension in. By the look of the rubbish in the boot, he's had half of Stanton Forest in there."

"And talking about the rev's car, I'd better get on with it before I lose what little light is left."

Not giving Ant the chance to protest, he guided his friend out of the dingy office with a matey clash of shoulders and walked Ant back to his car.

"By the way, Ant, did that roof sealer do its job on your Morgan?"

He guessed by Ant's crossed-fingered gesture that it had.

"I hope so. Lyn will flatten me if this thing leaks all over her again. It's already cost me one hairdo."

Fitch laughed.

"Serves you right. I hope it was expensive."

"Have you any idea how much women spend in those places?"

Fitch raised his eyebrows and shook his head.

"You mean more than the fiver I spend with Barry the Butcher?"

Ant let go of the door handle and turned back towards Fitch.

"Lord. Is he still in business? I assumed the council had closed him down as a danger to men's necks and earlobes years ago."

Memories of several run-ins with Barry caused Fitch to pick at a small scar on his chin, inflicted when the barber momentarily lost concentration scanning *The Racing Times* instead of paying attention to Fitch's flesh.

"Let's just say they have banned him from using cut-throat razors on anyone other than himself. And the times I've been in there, and he's covered in plasters, well..."

Both men laughed.

"Well," said Ant as he climbed into the Morgan, closed the door, and wound down his window, "at least he's come to his senses."

Fitch shook his head again.

"Er, no. Since he got the shakes, his wife petitioned the council. It was her that got him banned from using anything sharp on paying customers. Couldn't get the insurance, you see."

Ant was impressed at Fitch's graphic mime of sitting in the barber's chair, quaking, waiting for Barry to strike.

"Fancy meeting for dinner tonight? My treat, so we can catch up on things."

Ant offered the invitation more in hope than expectation. It was half term, and he knew Lyn guarded her downtime jealously.

"Trust you. I've just started playing my *Midsomer Murders* box set." Ant strained to hear Lyn as her voice faded in and out.

And politicians bang on about getting us superfast broadband. I'd settle for a decent mobile signal.

He moved location a couple of feet, extended his arm as high as it would reach, and shouted into the handset.

"Is that any better? Can you hear me now?"

He could tell Lyn was having none of it.

"I said, *Midsomer Murders*. Do you understand?"

Ant chose to act dumb.

"It's a bad signal, Lyn. See you at the Wherry Arms: seven thirty okay?"

He didn't wait for an answer. He calculated Lyn's response might contain several Anglo-Saxon words that he considered unbecoming of a head teacher.

"Hello... hello. Ant, can you hear me?"

Ant could hear her well enough but chose not to acknowledge the stream of invectives that followed.

Head teacher, indeed.

15

BATTLE OF WILLS

"Fish pie and an orange squash isn't exactly what I expected when you said you'd treat me."

Ant flinched.

I'm still in her bad books.

As the pair collected their meals from the bar and settled into a corner table of the packed pub, Ant hoped changing the subject might get him off the hook.

"How was the box set?"

"Twelve strangled, thirteen poisoned, sixteen drowned, plus four killed by bow and arrow. Oh, and six decapitated, if you must know."

Not bothering to add any inflection indicated to Ant that she'd decided to make him pay for disturbing her "me" time.

"Even more dangerous than Stanton Parva, eh, Lyn?"

Better keep quiet for a minute or two, I think.

Ant decided not to bite on Lyn's shake of the head and dismissive hand gesture as she lowered her gaze to bite on a forkful of fish pie.

I hope her pie's nicer than when I had it yesterday, or I'll really be in for it.

He took a long slug of his Fen Bodger pale ale before deciding to try his luck and push on.

It was never going to end well.

"And that's another thing. Why do you always wait until I have a mouth full of food?"

He watched as Lyn spat some of the pie back onto her plate.

"It didn't go well, then?"

"Which, the fish or my meeting with Reverend Morton?"

Ouch.

"I felt such a fool. There was a woman in the church kitchen getting things ready for the weekly coffee morning. I see she's upset, so I turn on the sympathy."

Ant tried hard not to look too confused.

"And...?"

"The vicar comes in and gives me daggers. It's as if I've stolen the church silver. It turns out the woman has recently lost her husband, and he's been visiting her each day to bring God's comforts."

Ant watched Lyn pick at her meal.

Perhaps she's not hungry after all.

"Seems a bit odd."

Ant didn't feel he deserved the daggers she gave him.

"What, the fish or the vicar?"

Not again.

"The vicar, Lyn. The vicar."

She shrugged her shoulders.

"It was as if I'd invaded their privacy. It was quite creepy, actually. When I tried to placate the reverend, the woman went for me. Perhaps she thought I was having a go at him. I don't know."

Lyn stopped talking just long enough to take a sip of her orange juice

"It seems he's been delivering food and stuff to keep her going. Logs for her wood burner and the like. She said he'd damaged his car getting to her cottage, and she felt guilty. That's when *he* got agitated, so I left them to it."

"Well, well," said Ant.

"Why so happy? I thought you had the vicar in the frame for Ethan's murder. Anyhow, how did you get on with Grindle?"

Lyn's renewed enthusiasm for the case energised Ant. He guzzled the last of his pint then looked at the empty glass as if inspecting a diamond for clarity.

"To answer your second enquiry first. Yes, I eventually caught up with him by mobile. Whether he's involved or not, I can't yet say. But I did pick up a nugget of information from the call."

Now that's got you puzzled.

"As for your assertion, you're correct. I thought the vicar was up to his neck in Ethan's death. It turns out the archbishop has threatened closure. Perhaps Morton thought he could prove the parish still held title to the cottage so he could flog it off to solve the church's financial problems."

Ant saw that Lyn was itching to speak.

"Are you saying the vicar didn't have any interest in Ethan's place?"

"Oh, I'm sure it crossed his mind. A man of God he may be, but he's still human."

The two friends exchanged conspiratorial glances.

"So where do we go now?"

Ant leant in and began to whisper.

"Until I get the answer to a hunch I'm following, let's just say the jury is out... or perhaps in the case of the good reverend, the keys to the pearly gates remain just out of reach."

Suddenly a pair of hands appeared as if from nowhere to scoop two empty glasses from the table.

"What are you two up to? You look like you're planning a bank robbery or something."

Ant looked around to see Bud, the landlord, smiling at them.

"Shush, keep your voice down. We don't want everyone to know," replied Ant, winking at Bud, who tapped the side of his nose with a nicotine-stained finger.

"Fair enough. Your secret's safe with me. Now, Lyn. How was that lovely fish pie?"

Ant tried not to look at Lyn, who was about to respond when Bud scuttled off without waiting for an answer to his question.

Thank heavens for that.

"Now, what did you say? Oh, yes. What do we do next?"

Ant retrieved a long white envelope from his inside pocket and withdrew the contents. He handed a folded sheet of paper to Lyn.

"That hunch I mentioned, well, what you've just told me about the vicar clarifies one or two things. But I'm not sure it's enough to put him in the clear."

He watched impatiently as Lyn unfolded the paper and carefully placed it on the table, flattening the folds with a firm palm.

"Well? What do you reckon?"

Lyn sank back into her chair and pointed to the bottom section of the page.

"Do you mean..."

Ant focused on Lyn's finger.

"Yes, almost certainly."

"But, Ant, he's as gentle a soul as you could wish to meet!"

He could see Lyn's distress.

"He's broke, Lyn. As for murder? We're all capable. It just needs the right set of circumstances to align and... *boom*. Believe me, I've seen it too many times."

Ant's voice had a ring of sad resignation. Now he wasn't thinking of Ethan. Instead, Ant was smack dab in the middle of a war zone in some godforsaken corner of the world.

"We do have to tell the police, don't we?"

Lyn's question snapped him back to the present.

"Not on your nelly. That fool, Riley, will make two and two add up to any number he wants to fit his reading of the 'facts.'"

Ant looked at Lyn in surprise as she threw her hands up.

"You're not making any sense."

Bud appeared at their table again.

"Coffee?"

Neither answered. It was all Ant could do not to tell Bud to shove off for interrupting his flow. In any event, the landlord got the message and shuffled from the table, muttering about miserable customers.

Relative solitude restored, the pair resumed their urgent conversation.

"The problem is, Riley has also got this information. My contact at the probate office told me he'd been sniffing around. My bet is that he's come to almost the same conclusion."

"Almost?"

"Don't look so puzzled, Lyn. I've also had a tip-off from my mate in pathology that the police will pick up Brian first thing in the morning. We have to be at that yard, but I've still got a couple of phone calls to make before I can be certain I'm right."

As they left the pub, Lyn repeated her question.

"Almost?"

Ant smiled.

16

IN A KNOT

Wednesday morning broke with a cold drizzle beneath a heavy grey sky. Ant pondered how the next hour or so would develop as he waited in the Morgan outside Lyn's cottage.

He waved at Lyn as she checked the lock had engaged, gave the front door one last pull, and crossed the pavement to the open car door.

Before Ant even had time to say hi, three police cars shot past—lights blazing, sirens screaming.

"Get in, Lyn. It's about to kick off."

She did as he requested, banged the door shut, and waited.

Blast this stupid car.

Instead of the Morgan purring to life, it sat motionless, engine refusing to engage. Ant turned the key again.

No joy.

"Sod it."

A frustrated Ant flung open his door, undid the leather strap holding the bonnet shut, and bad-temperedly folded it aside. Head disappearing into the engine bay, he muttered harsh words to his beloved car.

Two minutes passed.

Nothing.

Then.

"Yes. Fixed it."

Closing the bonnet, he secured the strap, jumped into the driver's seat like a gazelle escaping its tormentor, and turned the ignition key.

The Morgan roared to life.

"Bloody distributor cap," said Ant as he pulled away from the kerb and raced towards Wilcox Removals.

Ant noticed Lyn was about to speak.

"Don't ask."

His look was nearly enough.

"Serves you right for not fixing it before. You know it's been playing up for weeks."

Why do you always state the obvious?

He knew there was little point in defending himself, since, as usual, Ant knew she was right.

By the time they arrived at the yard, pandemonium had broken out. Ant saw Detective Inspector Riley standing in the middle of the yard flanked by six officers. Brian Wilcox stood immediately in front of Riley, his arms flailing, and shouting incoherently. Fitch was also there doing his best to calm things down.

"I wondered if you two might make an appearance. Well, you're wasting your time. We have our man."

Ant remained silent. Instead, he looked over towards Fitch.

"I heard the rumpus and thought the place was being burgled."

Ant nodded.

Simultaneously, the vicar appeared out of the ether, walked across the yard, and disappeared into the yard office without comment.

Ant looked on as Riley shook.

Doesn't take much to confuse you.

"Leave it," barked Riley as one of the officers made off towards the office. "I'll deal with him later."

Riley turned back to Wilcox. His body language gave off an air of a praying mantis about to strike.

"Brian Wilcox. I am arresting you for the murder of Ethan Baldwin—"

Wilcox wore a look of horror.

"But I had nothing to do with Ethan's death. What are you talking about?"

Ant moved closer as the two men exchanged increasingly angry words.

"You found out about the housing development."

"What are you talking about?"

"You also discovered Ethan had refused to sell Glebe Cottage to Grindle Developments."

It seemed to Ant that Riley was almost spitting his words out, such was his agitation.

"No, no," replied Wilcox, placing a hand on each side of his head.

Poor soul, thought Ant.

The onslaught continued.

"You discovered you were the closest living relative to Ethan Baldwin."

"Wha... what are you talking about?"

"You are broke. You've guaranteed everything you own to the bank."

"How do you know I'm—"

"Then you found out you were first in line to inherit

Glebe Cottage. All you had to do was get rid of Ethan and sell it to Grindle Estates, and—hey, presto—in one stroke, your financial difficulties would disappear in a puff of smoke."

Detective Inspector Riley raised his right arm and flicked his wrist in Wilcox's direction. Two officers covered the short distance between Riley and the hapless man. In a second, each had secured Wilcox's arms rendering him unable to move.

Stillness descended, the quiet broken only by a trickle of water overflowing from an ancient water butt, collecting rainfall from a broken downpipe of the ramshackle building it served.

Ant thought that had circumstances been different, the water trickle might have proved therapeutic. Not so today.

It was his confident voice that was the first to break the silence.

"You're almost there, Detective Inspector."

Ant chose his words with care.

He meant to taunt Riley.

He succeeded.

Ant observed Riley contort his face with hatred.

"Brian Wilcox did not murder Ethan Baldwin. Did he, Samantha?"

The shock unleashed by Ant's assertion was palpable. It was as if time had come to a stop.

He surveyed the unfolding scene.

Riley opened his mouth but spoke no words.

Fitch shook his head as if attempting to dislodge something too complicated to process.

Lyn looked as though a light bulb had just gone off in her head.

All eyes veered towards the yard office.

"Would you like to come out now?"

It seemed like an age before he detected movement.

Samantha rushed through an ill-fitting office door and made straight for her father. She wrapped her arms around him, forcing the two policemen to give way. They looked towards Riley. He gestured for them to stand down.

"Vicar, perhaps you should also join us."

Reverend Morton complied with Ant's assertive invitation.

Ant began to speak, his voice gentle, but no less in command of the situation.

"Samantha, when I came across you in church the other day, you said that Ethan and you told each other everything. I wonder if that included Ethan telling you about his childhood, about the orphanage. Am I correct, Samantha?"

She clung to her father, face pressed hard into his chest. Brian tenderly stroked his daughter's hair. Ant could see the man was racking his brains trying to make sense of events.

Samantha didn't answer. She turned towards Ant without making direct eye contact.

"Ethan told you about his burning need to discover who his parents were. And that as an adult he'd succeeded, at least in part."

Ant scanned the yard. Everyone's attention was focused on him.

"Eventually, he traced his mother. She lived in the village, didn't she?"

Samantha remained silent, her head still buried in her father's chest.

"Well, I'll be—"

"I know, Fitch. Sounds fantastic, doesn't it?"

He watched his friend nod as he returned his attention to Samantha.

"By the time he traced her, she'd died. We can only imagine how devastating that must have been for him, yet he still moved back to the village all those years ago. It was as if he needed to be near where he was born and the memory of his mother."

Ant's flow was suddenly interrupted.

"You have proof of all this?"

"Look in the parish records, Reverend. Just as Ethan had. He discovered a burial record of someone with a name almost identical to the one the adoption agency gave him. Except it wasn't Matilda Baldwin. It was Matilda Baldwin-Wilcox."

Ant turned to Brian just as the man let out a gasp.

You never knew. What a tragedy.

"But we don't have any relatives. They're all dead. It's just Samantha and me. Just the two of us."

Ant gave Brian time to compose himself as he gave his daughter an extra squeeze.

"I'm afraid that's true... now."

He didn't mean to be cruel.

Samantha shifted position to face Ant, forcing her father to move with her, such was the grip she still had on him.

"You're a liar. I thought you were nice. But you're just like all the rest."

Ant shook his head slowly. Almost imperceptively.

"Your dad did a good job at hiding his money problems from you for a long time. But you found out. Banks don't care who they talk to when they ring. They just want their money back."

Ant moved towards Brian and his daughter. Brian had started to cry.

I bet you've never seen him do that before.

"Ethan became obsessed with proving the link between

him and your father, and therefore to you. A fact you fully exploited when you found out about Grindle Developments wanting his cottage. You told me in church that... how did you put it, 'someone was hassling Ethan.' Well, I think you made that up to cover your tracks. The truth is Ethan refused to help. Isn't that so?"

Ant saw Samantha begin to break away from her father.

"Not just yet, young lady. I think you lured Ethan to this yard on the promise of helping him complete his family tree. Perhaps you told him your father kept the old family records in the office safe. Once you had him in the privacy of the office, you pleaded with him again to help your father pay off his debts. After all, if he sold the cottage, he would have more than enough money. When he refused again, you killed him."

Ant met Samantha's eyes as they burned into him.

"You can't prove any of this, Anthony. What are you trying to do?"

Ant shot back at the clergyman.

"A man is dead, Vicar. A man you argued with and failed to support when he needed help."

Reverend Morton recoiled at Ant's accusation. His reaction told Ant that his assumption had been correct.

"I—I thought he was just making trouble because we argued about the church pews. How was I to know that?" The vicar lowered his head.

You might well do that.

Ant turned back to Samantha, keen to get this awful thing over with.

"You strangled him and put him on the tailgate of that van. He was an old, frail man. It didn't take much effort, did it? After all, the hydraulic tailgate did all the work."

He pointed towards the van Fitch had repaired.

"When you had his body inside, you drove to the woods and staged his suicide. It was clever of you to use the same rope to string him up that you'd used to strangle him, except it left two distinct burn marks. As for the knot—well, your training with the Sea Cadets came in handy in the end, didn't it?"

He watched as Samantha's mouth turned up slightly at the edges. It seemed only Ant noticed the smirk.

Brian Wilcox interrupted.

"That's rubbish. My daughter can't drive."

Ant smiled and looked at Lyn.

"Oh, but she can. We saw her the other night moving vans around the rear of your yard, Brian. The truth is, she drove to the woods, strung Ethan up, and spent some time literally covering her tracks—but not well enough."

Ant looked over to Riley.

"Detective Inspector, I know you will have matched the broken branches and depressions in the trackway to this van, correct?"

I hope you catch my drift and go for this, Riley.

Ant watched Riley squirm but quickly catch onto Ant's risky ruse. He nodded his head, although Ant knew the detective had done no such thing.

Riley pointed at two constables and flicked his finger in the direction of Stanton Woods. They required no further instruction, leaving the yard to check Ant's theory.

"Once you'd selected the tree, it was an easy enough job to reverse the van. You pulled Ethan back onto the tail lift, tied the rope around Ethan's neck, and secured the other end around the branch. It was then just a case of lowering the tail lift until Ethan swung free. Finally, you placed a log on its side underneath the poor man, and—what do you know—we have a suicide."

Samantha grimaced.

"Like the vicar said, you can't prove anything."

Ant shook his head.

"I'm afraid I can, Samantha."

As he spoke, the remaining two officers moved towards Samantha.

"You see, you got sloppy. Perhaps you were exhausted by then, but when you cut the rope to length, some of the remnants got caught in the hydraulic mechanism of the tail lift. I've had them analysed, Samantha. They match."

Ant could see he'd once more caught Riley off guard as the detective's face flushed with embarrassment.

"Oh, and then there's this..."

Ant retrieved a small plastic bag from his coat pocket and handed it to Riley.

"Please ignore my fingerprints when you have it dusted. I'm sure you will find Miss Wilcox's prints all over it. We found that pen in Glebe Cottage."

Ant watched Riley bristle.

Here we go.

"What were you doing in—?"

He knew the detective wanted to grill him on how he came to be inside the cottage. Ant noted Riley had censored himself by thinking better of the idea. Instead, he accepted the plastic bag from Ant and read the inscription on the pen: Wilcox Removals and Storage.

"You made a right mess of Glebe Cottage looking for Ethan's will, Samantha. Then again, it was quite clever making it look like a burglary. Pity you weren't more careful about what you left behind," added Ant.

He could see Lyn itching to catch his attention.

"But what about Grindle Developments?"

"Quite right, Lyn. You recall me saying last night I had a

couple of calls to make? Well, I got back in touch with Stephen Grindle and probed our earlier conversation a little deeper. He told me a young woman contacted him to suggest a deal involving Glebe Cottage. He thought it was a hoax and didn't take things any further."

Ant looked back towards Riley.

"I'm sure he'll confirm what I've said, Detective Inspector. I have his number if it would help."

Ant sensed the irritation he was causing Riley.

He brought his attention back to Samantha.

"Now, is that enough proof?"

Hardly had he stopped speaking before the young woman let go of her father and raced towards Ant, her fists flailing. Two constables reacted in an instant to restrain her.

He found Samantha's facial expression hard to comprehend as her contorted features bore down on him. She had changed beyond all recognition as she spat her words at Ant.

"It was his fault. I tried being nice, but he wouldn't help. He could have stopped my dad going to jail. I lost my mum when I was a kid. I'm not going to lose my dad as well. Well, now he'll inherit Ethan's estate, and when Dad is released, he'll never have to worry about money again."

This time it was Ant's turn to be confused. He looked around trying to get a grip on why she'd talked about prison. Then he noticed Fitch closing his eyes and tilting his head backwards.

"I'm guessing your daughter is talking about the tachograph, Brian? When I repaired your van, I noticed something odd about the tachograph in the cab. Have you been doctoring it to extend your driving hours above the legal limit because you couldn't afford to hire a driver?"

Brian nodded then lowered his head.

"Oh, Samantha. What have you done?"

Ant looked on as Father and Daughter exchanged a final look before Samantha was placed in the back of a police Jaguar and driven away.

Didn't even look back at your father.

Ant gestured for Lyn to comfort Wilcox as he stood alone in the suddenly desolate yard. He knew that, in truth, there was little she could do or say.

At the yard gate, Ant chatted to Fitch and the vicar, each trying to make sense of the tragedy that had unfolded before them.

"Even if Wilcox has been fiddling with his driving hours, he won't get a custodial sentence for a first offence. Not that it matters. He's lost his business anyway, poor man."

Fitch nodded in agreement.

"But what about the inheritance when Glebe Cottage is sold?"

Ant was quick to respond.

"Ethan has left it all to the charity who brought him up. Isn't that right, Reverend?"

The vicar nodded.

"What?" exclaimed Fitch.

"It's true. As Ethan's executor, I met their representative the other day. They needed some information that I was able to provide."

Ant joined his two companions in a few seconds of reflective silence.

"One man dead, two lives ruined," said Fitch.

"WHAT I DON'T UNDERSTAND IS why the vicar was coming out of Ethan's place?"

Ant was distracted, hoping the Morgan would behave itself as he drove Lyn back to her place.

"Oh, you mean the papers your secretary saw him with, Lyn? Well, it seems Ethan typed the reverend's sermon each week. The vicar panicked when he realised last Sunday's was still in Glebe Cottage, so he retrieved it to ready for Sunday."

"Who's a clever chap, then."

He basked in the reflected glory of Lyn's compliment as he felt her hand flatten the collar of his waxed jacket.

Suddenly she recoiled.

"What's the matter?"

He was aware Lyn was giving him daggers.

"I thought you said you'd fixed the leak in this stupid car?"

Ant looked at the roof seam above Lyn's left shoulder.

"I have," he answered with misplaced confidence.

"Then why have I got a wet bottom?"

END

GLOSSARY

UK English to American English

- **Back garden:** Yard
- **Bap:** Bread roll
- **Banging on:** Slang term for someone who keeps repeating point of view time after time. E.g "He bangs on about the cost of gas every time I see him."
- **Bob cap:** A knitted, woollen head covering with a "bobble" (ball shape) attached to the top
- **Bobbie:** Cop
- **Booby:** Slang word, a mistake: "I made a booby of that."
- **Box van:** A truck with a hard shell to carry goods in
- **Bozo:** Slang for a stupid person: "You are a bozo."
- **Broad:** A stretch of water formed from old peat diggings. Common in Norfolk and Suffolk regions of the UK. Can take the form of narrow

stretches of water, like canals or open water, or small lakes.

- **Buttercross:** Medieval term used to describe a standing cross, or open-sided small building, where foodstuffs and other goods were exchanged, usually in villages or small towns.
- **Car bonnet:** Hood
- **Chav:** Derogatory slang for a young person wearing designer clothes with a brash manner
- **Chippy:** Traditional British family-run, fast-food outlet selling fish (usually cod and haddock) with fries and a selection of sides including peas, gravy, sausages, pies, chicken, and burgers
- **Clocked us:** To be seen. "Quick, let's go, they've clocked us"
- **Cottoned on:** To eventually understand something, "The police have cottoned on to us."
- **Did a flit:** Ran off, or more usually, to disappear from a building without notice
- **Digestive biscuit:** Also known as a sweet meal biscuit
- **Dunke(d):** To dip a biscuit into a hot drink (usually tea)
- **Fag:** Slang word for cigarette
- **Fine fettle:** In good order/health. "You look in fine fettle today."
- **Gob:** Street slang for a loudmouth, usually said in a derogatory way
- **Goodnight Vienna:** Slang term for "It's all over." E.g. "One more mistake like that, and it's goodnight Vienna."
- **Greasy spoon:** An affectionate term to describe a

privately owned roadside, fast-food outlet, or downtown food outlet

- **Happy as Larry:** "Larry" is thought to be of Australian boxer Larry Foley (1847 - 1917). He never lost a fight and retired at 32 collecting £1,000 for his final fight.
- **Hostelry:** Nickname for a British pub
- **Knocking Shop:** A place of ill repute: Brothel
- **Lay-by:** A safe place to pull over on the highway
- **Lorry:** A truck
- **Mint Humbug:** Black-and-white, striped, boiled candy
- **Mitts:** Slang. "Get your mitts (hands) off me."
- **Mobile phone:** Cell phone
- **Plod:** Nickname for a policeman or "the police"
- **Plonked:** Plunk(ed)
- **Postie:** A postman/woman
- **Quid:** Slang for a British pound. "Can you lend me ten quid?"
- **Scrumping:** Taking apples from a tree, usually without permission
- **Skip:** Debris box. Also known as skip boxes in some US states
- **Snug:** A small room in an old-fashioned British pub
- **Squaddie:** A private in the British army
- **Tallyman:** A person who sells goods and/or collects weekly cash payment by calling at the buyer's property: a form of credit.
- **Tiff:** Lighthearted argument, often between couples
- **Wellies or Wellingtons:** Rain boots. Footwear

that extend to just below the knee. Usually used
for walking or country sports in poor weather.
Said to have been named after the Duke of
Wellington.

DID YOU ENJOY DEATH BY HANGING?

Reviews are so important in helping get my books noticed. Unlike the big, established authors and publishers, I don't have the resources available for big marketing campaigns and expensive book launches (though I live in hope!).

What I *do* have is the following of a loyal and growing band of readers.

Genuine reviews of my writing help bring my books to the attention of new readers.

If you enjoyed this book, it would be a great help if you could spare a couple of minutes and head over to my Amazon page to leave a review (as short or long as you like). All you need do is click on one of the links, below.

    UK

    US

Thank you so much.

JOIN MY READER'S CLUB

Getting to know my readers is the thing I like most about writing. From time to time I publish a newsletter with details on my new releases, special offers, and other bits of news relating to the Norfolk Murder Mystery series. If you join my Readers' Club, I'll send you this gripping short story free and ONLY available to club members:

A Record of Deceit: 17,000 word short story

Grace Pinfold is terrified a stranger wants to kill her. Disturbing phone calls and mysterious letters confirm the threat is real. Then Grace disappears. Ant and Lyn fear they have less than forty-eight hours to find Grace before tragedy strikes - a situation made worse by a disinterested Detective Inspector Riley who's convinced an innocent explanation exists.

Character Backgrounds: A 7,000 word insight

Read fascinating interviews with the four lead characters in the Norfolk Cozy Mysteries series. Anthony Stanton, Lyn Blackthorn, Detective Inspector Riley and Fitch explain what drives them, their backgrounds and let slip an insight into each of their characters. We also learn how Ant, Lyn and Fitch first met as children and grew up to be firm friends - even if they do drive each other crazy most of the time!

You can get your free content by visiting my website at www.keithjfinney.com

I look forward to seeing you there.

Keith

For Joan who is always there for me.

ACKNOWLEDGMENTS

Cover design by Books Covered

Edit & Proofreading: Paula.
paulaproofreader.wixsite.com/home

ALSO BY KEITH FINNEY

In the Norfolk Murder Mystery Series:

Dead Man's Trench (UK) (US)

Narky Collins, Stanton Parva's most hated resident, lies dead in the bottom of an excavation trench. Was it an accident, or murder?

Amateur sleuths, Ant and Lyn, team up to untangle a jumble of leads as they try to discover the truth when jealousy, greed and blackmail combine into an explosive mix of lies and betrayal.

Will the investigative duo succeed, or fall foul of Detective Inspector Riley?

The Boathouse Killer

Geoff Singleton was wealthy, successful and hadn't a care in the world, having recently married the love of his life, Hanna.

Except someone murdered him.

A jealous boyfriend from Hanna's past is seen in the village.

An investor in the victim's investment company stands to lose a fortune.

Fake police officers throw their weight around.

Yet Detective Inspector Riley refuses to believe anything untoward has happened.

Emotions run high as Ant and Lyn work to prove Riley wrong and find Geoff's killer... before they strike again.

Website

Facebook

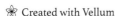 Created with Vellum

Printed in Great Britain
by Amazon

39151828R00087